PUFFIN CANADA

TROUBLE IN PARADISE

ERIC WALTERS is the highly acclaimed, bestselling author of more than sixty novels for children and young adults. His books have won the Silver Birch and the Red Maple Awards, as well as numerous other prizes, including the White Pine, Snow Willow, Tiny Torgi, Ruth Schwartz and IODE Violet Downey Book Awards. His novels have also received honours from the Canadian Library Association Book Awards and the Children's Book Centre, and won UNESCO's international award for Literature in Service of Tolerance.

To find out more about Eric and his novels, or to arrange for him to speak at your school, visit his website at www.ericwalters.net.

Also by Eric Walters from Penguin Canada

CAMP X
TROUBLE IN PARADISE

ERIC WALTERS

PUFFIN
CANADA

PUFFIN CANADA

Published by the Penguin Group

Penguin Group (Canada), 90 Eglinton Avenue East, Suite 700, Toronto, Ontario, Canada M4P 2Y3
   (a division of Pearson Canada Inc.)

Penguin Group (USA) Inc., 375 Hudson Street, New York, New York 10014, U.S.A.
Penguin Books Ltd, 80 Strand, London WC2R 0RL, England
Penguin Ireland, 25 St Stephen's Green, Dublin 2, Ireland (a division of Penguin Books Ltd)
Penguin Group (Australia), 250 Camberwell Road, Camberwell, Victoria 3124, Australia
   (a division of Pearson Australia Group Pty Ltd)
Penguin Books India Pvt Ltd, 11 Community Centre, Panchsheel Park, New Delhi – 110 017, India
Penguin Group (NZ), 67 Apollo Drive, Rosedale, Auckland 0632, New Zealand
   (a division of Pearson New Zealand Ltd)
Penguin Books (South Africa) (Pty) Ltd, 24 Sturdee Avenue, Rosebank, Johannesburg 2196, South Africa

Penguin Books Ltd, Registered Offices: 80 Strand, London WC2R 0RL, England

First published in Puffin Canada paperback by Penguin Group (Canada),
   a division of Pearson Canada Inc., 2010
Published in this edition, 2011

1 2 3 4 5 6 7 8 9 10 (OPM)

LIBRARY AND ARCHIVES CANADA CATALOGUING IN PUBLICATION

Walters, Eric, 1957–
   Trouble in paradise / Eric Walters.

(Camp X)

ISBN 978-0-14-317470-7

1. World War, 1939–1945—Secret Service—Juvenile fiction. I. Title. II.
   Series: Walters, Eric, 1957– . Camp.

PS8595.A598T76 2011   jC813'.54   C2011-903120-5

Visit the Penguin Group (Canada) website at www.penguin.ca

Special and corporate bulk purchase rates available; please see
www.penguin.ca / corporatesales or call 1-800-810-3104, ext. 2477 or 2474

TROUBLE IN PARADISE

CHAPTER ONE

"QUIET, PLEASE!" Miss Hilroy yelled.

The noise level in the classroom dropped, but it was still far from quiet. The boys at the back—a pack of seven—pretended they hadn't heard her.

"Now!" she screamed as she slammed the yardstick against the top of her desk.

That shut everybody up, although I was pretty sure that if Miss Hilroy didn't start to use that yardstick on a couple of those boys' palms, it would soon have no more effect than her voice. Then again, she was so old and frail I wasn't sure a hit from her would even leave a mark.

"That's better," she said. "We have a few minutes left before the end of our day—the end of our week—and I want to use that time productively."

"Mr. Hutton always let us slack off for the last few minutes of the day," one of the boys said.

"Mr. Hutton was *my* student before he was *your* teacher, and as I recall from his marks, I am not surprised that he advocated slacking off," she said. "And further, he is no longer your teacher, and as long as I'm in charge, you shall do as *I* say."

She was trying to sound forceful, but instead her voice squeaked over the last few words. It wasn't her fault. She stood no more than five feet tall and weighed less than a hundred pounds, and I didn't even want to hazard a guess as to her age. From what I'd heard, she'd been a teacher here practically forever before she retired—which was a long time ago—and had been pressed back into service when Mr. Hutton was summoned to become part of the Bermuda Home Guard.

There was some snickering from the back of the room, and I heard a hint of somebody imitating her voice. Miss Hilroy, who was as deaf as she was old, didn't hear a thing, and everybody else in the class pretended not to hear her being mocked.

"I thought that for the newest member of our class— joining eight others from off-island this year—we should take some time to learn a little bit of Bermuda history," she continued.

"She should know everything about it—she's *been* here for practically all of it," somebody muttered from the back.

"I'm sorry, could you repeat what you said?" she asked. "I'm a little hard of hearing."

"I said that would be rather a bore for the rest of us who already know Bermuda, don't you think?" one of the boys, Phillip, said.

"Yes, perhaps you could provide them with private tutelage," his friend Thomas added.

We were all wearing the same uniform—grey flannel pants, white dress shirt, blue blazer and school tie, and pretty much the same for the girls, except with a skirt—so it was hard to tell these guys apart, but Phillip and Thomas had already made an impression on me, a smart-alecky one. Both of them had *very* formal British accents—much stronger than the local Bermudian accent. And not only did they like to talk, they liked to use big fancy words and to pronounce normal words in a fancy way. When I said "privacy" with a long *i* sound like in "pirate," they laughed and said it was "pr*i*vacy" with a short *i* like in "principal."

They were both annoying show-offs. Plus, they were two of the other seven students who were new to the school, like me, so I didn't know why they thought they knew so much about Bermuda. They'd been sent here from their homes in England to avoid the Nazi bombing, the Blitz. If there were seven in my class, then there must be dozens more spread throughout the school. Some had come with their families—at least their mothers and siblings—and others had been shipped over to live with strangers. That would have been hard.

I already knew a thing or two about Bermuda. Not being a big fan of surprises, as soon as I'd found out we were going to be coming here, I'd looked it up in the encyclopedia at school. Bermuda was a British territory, ruled by a governor appointed by the king of England. Most of the people I'd met so far had British backgrounds, which I guess explained the accents. Although Bermuda seemed like some kind of island paradise, it wasn't really remote, being not that far from the United States, off the coast of North Carolina.

"Well, then, perhaps, rather than telling our newest classmate about Bermuda, our very newest classmate could tell us all about himself," she suggested.

There was a chorus of groans. I would have groaned myself if she hadn't been looking straight at me.

"Please, George, tell us about yourself."

"Um … there isn't much to tell," I mumbled.

"Please, come to the front."

Reluctantly, I got to my feet and went to the front of the class.

"My name is George," I said.

"Please, louder," she said.

"My name is George!" I said in my loudest indoor voice.

"Please state your *last* name, and speak more clearly," Miss Hilroy said. "There's nothing to be nervous about."

Yes there was. Standing in front of a group of people and talking was about the most terrifying experience in the world, which, of course, was strange considering what I'd already faced in my life.

"Tell you what, we'll make it as though you're talking on the wireless," she said, adding gleefully, "Isn't it wonderful that we have a wireless radio station now?"

Bermuda had just gotten its first radio station—it was because of the war and the need to communicate with everybody if there was an emergency.

"I'll ask you questions and you provide the answers," she said. "That should be good fun!"

We obviously had different ideas of fun.

"So, George, begin with your name, age and siblings, if any."

"Yes, ma'am. My name is George Braun and I'm twelve. My brother, Jack, is fifteen and he goes to this school, too. My family moved here ten days ago."

"Where did your family move from?" Miss Hilroy asked.

"We're Canadians. We lived on a farm in Ontario—"

"A farm ... that explains the smell of manure," Phillip said, and some of the others chuckled.

I felt my fingers start to ball into fists. I should just let it pass and— One of the boys made a low mooing sound and a second snorted like a pig.

"That's *so* funny," I said sarcastically. "I'm glad the boys at the back know their animal sounds ... although making little comments when I'm not looking directly at you might mean you should make a chicken sound instead."

I stared right at Phillip and the smile was wiped off his face.

"We moved closer to the action, not away from it," I went on. Bermuda wasn't like the front lines in Europe, but planes did refuel here, and there were U-boats out there somewhere in the Atlantic. "Any of you have anything you want to add?" I asked, looking from one to the other. They all looked down at the ground.

After everything I'd been through, I wasn't about to take any back talk from a bunch of seventh-grade snobs. The best way to handle bullies was to stare them down.

"I'm sorry, George, I don't understand what you're saying ... could you speak up?" Miss Hilroy asked.

"I was just asking if the gentlemen at the back of the room had any questions, but they appear to have nothing more to say," I said.

"Oh, good, but if there *are* any questions, please raise your hand. And what was the reason for your family coming to our island?"

"We're here in Bermuda now because my father was reassigned. He was with the St. Patrick's division, chasing

Rommel across North Africa. He's a captain and received medals for bravery, and he was wounded in action."

Nobody had any smart-aleck comment to that one.

"You must be very proud of him," Miss Hilroy said.

"We're all proud of him. He's been stationed here as part of the defence of the harbour, and my mother is also helping out with the war effort. She's working in Hamilton with the Department of Censorship."

"So both your parents are making contributions to the war effort," she said.

"Yes" was my simple reply. What I wanted to say—but of course never would, because for one thing I was sworn to silence under the Official Secrets Act—was that both my brother and I had fought Nazi spies in Canada, and that we weren't just a couple of stupid kids sitting at the back of a class making dumb remarks. We'd done things to save lives. We'd done things that had cost the lives of Nazis ... done them personally. Not only could I not tell them that, I didn't even want to think about it. It had already cost me enough sleep.

"Thank you, George, for telling us a bit more about your family. It is now three o'clock and time for dismissal," Miss Hilroy announced.

The class came alive with noise as kids started talking and laughing, gathering up their things and heading quickly to the doors. I felt pretty happy myself. It was

Friday, I'd made it through my first week, and Dad was going to be home on a two-day pass. The room quickly began to empty. I wasn't in a hurry. It was better to just let those boys leave. No point in pushing harder—although part of me wondered if they might be waiting for me outside. Seven to one wasn't the best odds, but I'd faced worse.

"Don't let them get to you," one of the girls—her name was Lesley—said. Besides Miss Hilroy, we were the only two people left in the room.

"What?"

"The lot at the back. Don't take it personally."

She had a very gentle accent. She smiled, and I felt myself starting to blush. I put my books in my bag, slung it over my shoulder and we walked to the door and out of the class. I took a quick look around. Nobody was waiting. Kids were scattered across the playing field, heading home. It was sunny and warm outside—not hot, but nothing like Canada in December.

"Those blokes feel like they're better than us Onions," Lesley said.

Now I was just confused. "Onions?"

She laughed. "That's what we call ourselves ... those who were born and raised on the island. We're Onions ... you know, like Bermuda Onions."

"Okay, but I'm not an Onion."

"Do you think you're better than *us* because you're from *Canada?*" she asked, suddenly sounding annoyed.

"No, of course not, it's just … just … we don't think we're better than anybody."

"So maybe they're right in treating you badly if you're not better than anybody," she said.

"But we're not worse … we're all the *same* where I come from."

"But not where *they* come from," she said. "Every Englishman thinks he's better than every colonial, whether it's somebody from Canada or Bermuda. But that lot thinks they're better than almost every Englishman, too."

"They don't seem that special to me," I said.

"That's because you don't know who they are."

"I don't care who they are," I said. I paused. "Who are they?"

"I'm not really sure, it's all pretty hush-hush, but I know they have to be from pretty important families or they wouldn't be here."

"Again, I don't get it."

"Do you think that ordinary people can send their children away to Bermuda to get away from the Blitz?"

"I hadn't really thought about it," I admitted. "But I don't care if the king of England sent over his kids, I—"

"Some of them *are* royalty," she said, cutting me off.

"They are?"

She nodded. "That's what I heard. You know, third and fourth cousin sort of things."

"I still don't care. We're all in this war together and we're all on the same side. Only Hitler thinks he's better than other people, and that's what we're fighting against."

"You don't seem to be afraid of a fight," she said.

"I'm not afraid of them. They're just a bunch of kids."

"And what are you, an old man of twelve?" she asked.

"No, it's just ... just ... I don't know."

If I'd told her the truth, she wouldn't have believed me. She would have thought I was either the biggest liar in the world or an escapee from the loony bin. Better to change the subject. The weather was usually safe. Or maybe the view? We were standing at the back of the playing field on a hill overlooking the ocean. Below us it stretched out in both directions as far as the eye could see.

"This sure is beautiful."

She shrugged her shoulders. "This?"

"Well ... yes. Don't you think?"

"I guess I really don't think about it much. This is just home."

"But ... look at the ocean," I said.

"Hard *not* to look at the ocean in Bermuda."

"I mean the colours." The water was bright blue in some places and emerald green in others.

"Honestly, I hardly notice."

"And the colours of the houses," I said. "It's as if a bunch of kids with crayons decided what they should look like." The houses were brilliantly painted in bright colours— reds, yellows, greens and blues in different combinations. Each was topped by a white ridged roof.

"Don't houses look like that where you're from?" Lesley asked.

"Not even close. They're mostly bricks and wood, and not painted like this."

We started down the path toward the beach. Most of the kids had already gone ahead of us.

"Which way do you go?" she asked.

I motioned to the left.

"Shame. I'm going the other way or I would have let you carry my books."

I was too stunned even to attempt a reply.

"There's my brother," I said, gesturing to where he was waiting up ahead. He was standing with a girl.

"He's cute. Too bad it looks like he's already taken."

"I don't know about the taken part, but cute has never been a word I've used to describe him."

"No, he's definitely a looker," she said. "Must run in the family."

I started, and she gave me a little smile. I quickly looked away.

Jack saw me coming down the path and gave a dirty look, which I knew meant he didn't want me to come any closer.

"I'm going to wait here for a minute," I said.

Lesley stopped beside me, but gave me a questioning look.

"You know ... so he can have some privacy."

"That's considerate."

"Yeah, considerate ... sure."

And smart. I didn't mind getting a bunch of grade sevens mad at me, but Jack was a different kind of animal. He had both a temper and the strength to make that temper count for something.

"Can I ask you a question?" Lesley asked.

"Of course."

"I know why those kids have come from England, but why are you and your brother here?"

"Because our parents are stationed here ... like I said."

"But there are lots of soldiers and sailors stationed in Bermuda as part of the war effort, and as far as I know, none of them brought along *their* children."

"It's because we have both parents stationed here," I said. "And because they needed them both here, the deal was that we got to come along."

"Oh, I guess that makes sense."

That was our cover story, so it was *supposed* to make sense. It was certainly more believable than the truth: we had been relocated so that Nazi agents wouldn't be able to find us and would go on believing we'd been killed in a car crash. That was the story that had been cooked up for us. It had even been an article in *The Whitby Reporter*! Funny that it was so much easier to believe than what had really happened—that we'd foiled a Nazi plot to set off a massive explosion at a munitions plant. Sometimes the truth really is a lot stranger than fiction.

As we stood there and waited, Jack said something and the girl giggled and laughed. She put a hand on his shoulder and then, to my utter shock, gave him a little kiss on the cheek and a hug!

"Looks like you were wrong. He *is* taken," Lesley said.

The girl released Jack and headed off down the beach.

"Can we go now?" Lesley asked.

"Sure ... of course."

We started back down the path toward Jack.

"Are you going to introduce me to your brother?" Lesley asked.

"If you want, I can—" I stopped mid-sentence. Jack wasn't alone. Two other students, about his size and probably in his grade, suddenly appeared out of nowhere—and one of them pushed Jack! Before I could even think to react, Jack hauled off and punched the guy square in the face. He crumpled to the ground.

CHAPTER TWO

I RACED DOWN THE PATH. "Jack!" I screamed. "Jack!"

He didn't turn around. He kept his eyes on the two boys—one helping the other—running away down the beach.

"Jack, are you all right?" I yelled as I skidded to a stop beside him.

"I'm good, but it wasn't me who got punched. Might be a better question to ask him," he said, gesturing down the beach. The two boys were still moving away, although the one who hadn't been hit looked back anxiously over his shoulder.

"But why did you punch him?"

"He shoved me. Didn't you see?"

Lesley—who I'd completely forgotten about—stopped beside us.

"Um ... this is Lesley," I said. "And this is my brother, Jack."

14

"I could tell you two were brothers," she said.

"He doesn't look anything like me," Jack said. "I'm good-looking."

She laughed. "Not by the way you look, by the way you act."

Now Jack looked confused. "Has George been punching people?"

"Not punching—also not backing down. Those Brits don't seem to like either of you," she said.

"How did you know that guy was a Brit?" Jack asked.

"I know everybody in the school, and he's from away. So why did he shove you to begin with?" she asked.

"He said something about how I shouldn't be talking to that girl because she was of a different *station* ... whatever that means."

"It means that she's ruling-class English and you're a lowly colonial," Lesley said.

"I figured it didn't mean that she wasn't good enough for *me*," Jack said. "I told him to go take a hike and then he shoved me, so I popped him."

"We're supposed to stay out of fights," I said.

"Sounds like you were barking up the same tree," Jack said.

"Maybe, but I didn't actually fight anybody."

"Neither did I. I punched somebody and he ran away. That's hardly a fight."

"Besides, he started it," Lesley said.

"Hey, I like this girl," Jack said, and Lesley smiled. "All I did was finish the fight ... well ... maybe it's finished."

"Maybe?" I asked. "What else are you going to do?"

"*I'm* not going to do anything."

I understood what he meant. Maybe the guy who got punched would talk to his friends, and we didn't have any friends yet ... unless you counted Lesley. I figured she could probably deliver a pretty good punch.

"But even if he comes back with a couple of friends, I'm still okay. I don't mind being outnumbered three to one," Jack bragged.

"Don't you mean three to two?" Lesley said, pointing at me.

I waited for Jack to make some smart comment.

"Yeah, you have a point. My baby brother can handle himself. He could have probably taken the two of them without my help."

That wasn't what I'd expected him to say.

"Thanks."

"Sure ... but really ... how tough could they be if one punch sent them both packing?"

He had a point.

"We'd better get going, Georgie."

"Georgie?" Lesley asked.

"No, it's George. My name is George." Oh great, I thought, nothing like starting over in a new place and bringing your old baby nickname with you.

Jack laughed. "Right, he's George … but you call him Georgie if you want. Now, give your girlfriend a kiss goodbye, Georgie, and let's get on our way."

"She not my—"

Lesley reached over and kissed me on the cheek! And before I had a chance to react, she'd turned and was gone.

"Not a word!" I threatened Jack.

"Not a word," he agreed. "But maybe a little song. How does that go again? … uh … yes, I remember. *Georgie Porgie, pudding and pie, kissed the girls*—"

I took a swing at Jack, but he dodged away and I almost fell over.

"—*and made them cry!*" he continued.

"At least I'm pretty sure that Lesley isn't a German spy," I said.

Before I could regret my words, Jack grabbed me by my school blazer, spun me around and pulled me up on my tippytoes so I was facing him eyeball to eyeball.

"Want to repeat that?" he asked.

"Not really. I think I'm pretty sorry I said it the first time."

His angry look dissolved into a smile and he lowered me.

"I guess I deserved it," he said.

"Not really. I'm sorry."

Jack's last girlfriend—really, his first and only girl-friend—had turned out to be a Nazi agent who was really twenty-two years old. She'd lied about everything, start-ing with her age. But to be fair, we'd lied, too, in order to protect our family's cover story.

"Who was that girl you were with?" I asked.

"Her name is Louise. She's very nice. She's in my class."

"Maybe in your grade. According to those two guys, you're definitely *not* in her class," I joked. "I've got a bunch of them in my room who are just like that."

"I don't care where they come from or who they think they are," Jack said, "I just know I'm not taking it from anybody. And you make sure you don't either, understand?"

"I understand."

"Hey!" a voice came from behind.

We both turned. Coming down the beach were eight or nine boys, all in our school uniform. Leading the pack were two familiar faces—the guys who had run away. I felt a chill go down my spine. That's why they'd been running, to get help.

"We could run. They wouldn't catch us," I said.

"They wouldn't catch us today, but we'd still have to come to school on Monday. You get going … walk away and I'll make sure they don't go after you."

For a split second, I almost agreed. "No. I'm not going anywhere without you."

"Last chance," he warned me.

A noise caught my attention. Four more boys came out of the bushes behind us, blocking our getaway.

"Too late now," I said.

"Watch my back," Jack said.

The group slowly surrounded us. They knew they didn't have to rush because we had no place to go.

"Where do you get off?" one of them, the biggest and oldest, demanded as he stopped right in front of Jack, his arms crossed over his chest. "You think you can just go around talking to whoever you want?"

"I don't know. Right now it's like I have to talk to people I don't even want to talk to," Jack replied.

The big guy looked thrown by Jack's comment. He'd expected something different—maybe fear or an apology or Jack to back down or something. I was feeling enough fear for both of us, but I knew nobody was going to back down.

"Do you know that was somebody special you kissed?" he demanded.

"First off, I didn't kiss anybody, and second, unlike you, only somebody special would kiss me."

The boy looked shocked, and a few of the others snickered before he silenced them with a stare.

"And from the way he ran away after I punched him, I guess there must be somebody else who's really special," Jack said, "a special little girl, because no man would run away like that."

"Cheeky little blighter," he said. "You're going to regret your actions and your words. I'm here to teach you a lesson."

"Obviously you must not be much of a teacher if you need all these people to help."

"We stick together."

"Well ... let's see." Jack started counting them. "Twelve of you ... you sure you shouldn't send out for more, just in case?"

"I think we have quite enough to give you and this little pipsqueak the thrashing of your lives."

"Who are you calling a pip—?"

"Shut up, you little pipsqueak," Jack said, cutting me off. "She didn't kiss him, so let him go."

"He's not going anywhere. We're not letting him run for help."

"I don't need any help to take you down," Jack said. "But I guess you know that, or you wouldn't need eleven people to back you."

Why was Jack taunting them? He was just making them angrier ... then I realized what he was doing. He was try- ing to shame them, make them feel bad about it taking all of them to fight us. That could work—unless it only made them madder. Then again, how much madder could they get?

"So much for British fair play and all that garbage," I said. "You're nothing but a bunch of thugs. Good thing you're smart enough to know you need at least a dozen Brits to take on two Canadians."

"Brave talk, pipsqueak."

"He *is* brave," Jack said. "Brave enough not to need eleven guys to back him up. Tell you what, we'll rather *enjoy* fighting all twelve of you."

Before anybody could say anything more, Jack grabbed a piece of driftwood from the sand. Good plan, we both needed a weapon, and— He started drawing a line in the sand.

"Back up," Jack ordered, and some of the boys shifted as he drew a big circle with me right in the centre.

"We're going to fight all twelve of you, but two at a time ... starting with you," he said, pointing at the big guy who'd been doing all the talking, "and anybody else you want to bring into the ring with you ... unless you're afraid to fight a pipsqueak and his older brother ... who's still a couple of years younger than you."

"Do you really think I'm afraid of you?" he demanded.

"Actions speak louder than words. *I'm* not the one who's standing *outside* the ring. Pick who you want to come in with you. And then decide which two come in after we dispose of you and then the next two and the next two ... you get the idea."

"And why shouldn't we all jump you at once?" he asked.

"Like I said, if you don't have the guts to fight me alone, then that's what you'll do. I'm even giving you an advantage, because you get to choose somebody else to come with you and all I've got is this little seventh-grade pipsqueak. We'll wait here until you decide."

They gathered together and started talking.

I leaned in closer to Jack. "We can still make a break for it," I whispered.

"We're not going anywhere. No point in running."

"Do you really think we can beat them ... beat all of them?"

Jack laughed—that was the last thing I'd expected.

"We haven't got a *chance* of winning, but we're going to take a couple of them with us," he whispered in my ear.

The big guy, the bigmouth, came forward. With him was the second biggest of the group. They stepped into the circle.

"Let's set the rules," Jack said. "Anybody knocked unconscious or knocked out of the ring is out. Agreed?"

"Certainly," he agreed.

"Good. Let's get rid of these."

Jack pulled off his school jacket and began to undo his tie. He turned his back so he was facing me. "We both go for the loudmouth," he whispered. "I'll hit him high and you go low. Try to drive him out of the ring ... okay?"

I nodded.

Jack spun around and threw his jacket at the one guy and threw a punch at the second, who was too stunned to move out of the way. I hesitated for a split second and then lowered my head and charged at him. My head and shoulder hit him square in the stomach. Jack hit him again and he crumpled over, falling backward and outside the circle.

Jack turned to the remaining guy. He looked stunned ... no, scared.

"Look who's outnumbered now." Jack jumped forward and the guy leaped backward and out of the ring.

"Okay," Jack said. "Who's next?"

CHAPTER THREE

"HERE, TAKE THIS," my mother said as she pressed a cold cloth against my eye. Jack already had a cold cloth, holding it alternately to each of his eyes. We were sitting at the kitchen table, and very glad to be home.

"It's bad enough that one of you was in a fight, but both of you!" she said, shaking her head.

"It's not like we started it," I protested. Although, really, Jack did start it ... but he *did* get shoved first ... so maybe he didn't.

"People will think we're a bunch of savages," she said. "Here barely a week and already you've both managed to get into a fight. I think we should march over to the homes of those boys and you will both apologize to them."

"We don't even know all of them," Jack said.

"All of them?" she exclaimed. "How many were there?"

I looked at Jack and he looked at me.

"Answer my question," she said. Her tone left no doubt that she wanted an answer.

"Well ... there were a lot of people there," Jack said.

"You mean watching the fight?" she asked.

"*Some* of them were watching."

"Some? How many people did you two fight with?" She looked directly at me. "George?"

I wouldn't lie to my mother—not after all the things we already had to keep from her because of the Official Secrets Act.

"Six kids."

"Six people!" she exclaimed. "That's not a fight, that's a mob!"

"And we didn't know them because they were in older grades," I said.

"Older than your grade?" she asked.

"No, older than Jack's."

Now she looked horrified. "I'm going to contact the headmaster and possibly the police and—"

"But it wasn't like they were bigger than us, and we only fought them two at a time," Jack said.

"So you two were in three *separate* fights?" She sounded incredulous.

"Not really," Jack said. "It was all sort of the same fight ... we just took them on two at a time, that's all."

"What?" Now my mother sounded incredibly confused. I didn't blame her.

"The next two didn't start with us until we were finished with the two we were fighting," Jack explained.

"That ... that makes no sense."

"Those were the rules," Jack explained. "It made it, you know, more fair. It's not like we had to fight all six of them at once."

"But why would six boys want to fight you two?"

"Actually there were twelve of them," I pointed out.

Jack shot me a nasty look. "But we only *fought* six."

"Why would *twelve* boys want to fight you two? What did you do to bring this on?" This time she looked right at Jack.

"It wasn't his fault," I said, defending him. "Or mine. They wanted to fight us because Jack had talked to some girl that they thought he shouldn't talk to."

"All this trouble ... over a girl?"

"It wasn't about the girl," Jack said. "Not really. It was about people telling us they're better than us, telling us what to do. We're fighting the Nazis so people can't do that. Anyway, it's all over now."

"So tell me, did somebody—an adult—intervene, or did you all simply come to your senses?" our mother asked.

"No, it just got sorted out."

"And we're going to see them again on Monday morning ... at rugby practice," I said.

"They asked if we'd join the team," Jack explained.

"You two are going to play on the rugby team? You've never played rugby in your lives. Do you even know what the game is about?"

"We're not really sure," Jack said, "but they told us that the way we take and give a hit, we're bound to be naturals."

"They said they'd explain the rules to us as we go along."

Mom sat down at the table. She didn't look pleased.

"It did stop the fighting," I said, trying to make her happier about it all.

"I guess that's because we're sort of teammates now," Jack added.

She shook her head slowly. "Why didn't I have girls? Pummelling each other one minute and teammates the next. Sometimes boys and men make no sense to me at all."

"That's how I feel about girls," I said.

"At least they don't go around punching each other."

"I'd rather they just punched, instead of stabbing a guy in the back," Jack said, and we all knew what he meant— that girl, that spy, who had tricked him. That must have hurt far more than any punch.

"Not all girls are like Liesl," Mom responded.

"We know all girls aren't spies," Jack said.

"That's not what I meant. I mean, just because you were deceived once, don't look for deception from everybody."

That was easier said than done. After everything that had happened to us over the past months, I looked for spies, enemy agents, Nazis, secret codes and coincidences everywhere I went. I didn't even like somebody walking behind me. I checked behind doors and scanned every room I entered, just to make sure. When I read a newspaper, I looked for the Ireland Code, checking to see if the first letter of each word, when taken together, spelled out a secret message.

"The important thing is that it's over," Jack said.

"That's where you're wrong," my mother said.

"Aw, come on, Mom. You're not really going to make us apologize, are you?" Jack asked.

"Or call the headmaster or the police?" I added.

She shook her head. "No, but your father will be home soon, and he'll have more than a few things to say about this."

For the first time since he'd returned from overseas, I thought that it might be better if he were still in Africa. Jack didn't look any happier than I felt about our father speaking to us. Dad wasn't somebody who wasted a lot of words. Farmers were like that.

"Here, let me have a look at your eye," my mother said.

I lowered the cloth from my face.

"That's looking pretty bad."

"It feels pretty bad," I said.

"It's already coming up black and blue. It's going to look even worse by tomorrow. You've got yourself a first-class shiner," Jack said, and he laughed.

"You should talk. You have *two* black eyes."

"And some really sore ribs … at least I'm pretty sure my nose isn't broken, just a little swollen. But you know," he said, holding up his hand to look at the scrapes on his knuckles, "we gave as good as we got."

"Yeah, I guess we—"

"There is nothing to be proud about in this!" my mother said, cutting me off. "I can't even look at the two of you … it hurts my heart. I'm going to finish making supper, and you two need to go to your room and wait for your father to get home, so we can continue this discussion."

"When will supper be ready?" Jack questioned. "I'm really—"

"I haven't decided yet whether you two will be having supper. Now get to your room."

I sat on my bed, balancing the book on my lap. A little reading helped take my mind off the situation. And if I didn't move very much, it didn't hurt too badly. Not only my eye was sore, but also my jaw and places along both ribs. Slowly, deliberately, I balled the fingers of my right hand into a fist. That hurt, too, especially along the knuckles. The whole baby finger was swollen and felt as thick as the next one over. Sometimes punching hurt as much as being punched.

I eased myself up onto one elbow so I could see Jack. He was lying on his back, but his eyes were open, so I knew he wasn't sleeping.

"Jack?" I said quietly.

He didn't answer.

"Jack!"

"What?"

"I was wondering ... how mad do you think Dad is going to be?"

"Don't know. Pretty mad, I guess."

"But it really wasn't our fault," I said. "It's not like they were just going to let us walk away."

"Yeah, that's the truth."

I shifted around and stifled a little yelp from the jolt of pain in my ribs.

"George?" he said.

I looked over at Jack, who was now sitting on the edge of his bed.

"You done good," he said and gave me a smile.

He lay back down, as did I. Somehow, it didn't seem to hurt as much now.

CHAPTER FOUR

I WAS GETTING pretty hungry by the time I heard the sound I'd been waiting for—our front door opening and closing with a soft *click*, followed by my father's cheerful, "I'm home!" and his footsteps heading toward the kitchen. I wondered if I would ever get over the feeling of deep relief whenever I heard those sounds. They announced that all was right with the world again. I'd missed them during the time my father was fighting overseas. I smiled, and when I looked up, I could see that Jack was smiling softly, too.

And then came the sound we could have lived without: my mother's raised voice explaining, in exasperated tones, what "your sons" had been up to *now*. The poor guy barely had a chance to loosen his tie before getting the news of the day.

I climbed off my bed and went to the door so I could hear better—though I really didn't want to hear it.

"I know none of this has been easy for any of you, Betty ... all these moves. Tell you what, you go and make yourself a cup of tea and leave me to *deal* with the boys."

I didn't like the way he emphasized the word "deal."

"This needs to be a talk ... father to sons," he said. "No room here for a woman and her emotions. You just skedaddle."

They continued to talk, but all I could hear was a buzz of words.

"What are they saying?" Jack asked.

I shook my head. "I can't hear them right—" I heard footsteps down the hallway toward our bedroom. I ran back and got onto my bed, grabbing the book so it looked like I was reading.

"It's upside down!" Jack hissed.

I quickly spun the book right way up as the door opened, and suddenly there he was, filling the doorway.

"Dad!" I exclaimed. "It's good to—oww—" I groaned.

As I tried to stand up, my rib cage reminded me of what had happened and why I maybe shouldn't be so happy to see him.

"Where does it hurt?" he asked.

"It really doesn't hurt that much."

"Answer the question," he said sternly.

There wasn't much choice. "My side ... sort of my ribs and my hand," I said, holding up the right one. As I made a fist to show the scraped knuckles, even that hurt.

"What about your eye?" he demanded. "You can't honestly say that your eye isn't hurting."

"I was getting to it," I said.

He turned to Jack, who was sitting on the edge of his bed. "And you?"

"Pretty much the same ... and also the back of my head."

Dad came over and ran his hands over the back of Jack's head, feeling around.

"Ooowww!" Jack howled as he tried to draw away.

"There's half a goose egg back there," Dad said. "And quit squirming so I can see it."

He lowered Jack's head and parted the hair with his fingers. I could see Jack grimacing, trying not to react, but I had the feeling Dad wasn't being any too gentle.

"Your mother pretty well filled me in on the situation," our father said. "Not the best."

"No, sir," Jack said.

"No, sir," I parroted—no point in looking disrespectful here.

He took the chair from the desk and brought it over to between the beds, turned it around and sat backward on it.

"Your mother is pretty upset."

"We know," Jack said.

"I think my being gone and all of the moves have been very hard on her," he said. "Between the three of us, though, I think she's overreacting."

Overreacting? There were so many things we couldn't tell him about—the agents, the kidnappings, the tunnels, the guns and the threats ... and the deaths. If he'd known all of that, he'd have known why Mom wasn't *over*reacting as much as just *re*acting to what had happened.

"I told her that boys get into fights," he said. "Boys are boys."

Shockingly, it looked like this was going in the right direction, for us.

"And from what she told me, it wasn't really your fault," he said.

"Not really," Jack agreed.

"It's not like you started it ... did you?" he asked.

"No, sir," Jack replied. "They came after us and we didn't have any choice."

"That's what your mother said." He shook his head. "Six of them ... you fought six of them."

"Not each," Jack said, "that was between us."

He laughed. "Did I ever tell you about the time my brother, your uncle Jack, and I fought five guys at once?"

"No," Jack said. "I'd like to hear that story." After all, he was named after our father's older brother.

"Me too."

My father looked over at the door, like he was making sure it was still closed. He leaned in closer.

"You probably don't know it, but your uncle Jack has a fierce temper."

"Uncle Jack?" I questioned. He was always playing and joking around and making puns. I'd never seen him when he didn't have a smile on his face.

"Terrible temper," my father said. "Anyway, I was about your age, George, and I was pretty well minding my own business, playing with a ball in the schoolyard. These kids—there were five of them—took away my ball and started pushing me around."

"And you popped them?" Jack asked.

"Not me, your uncle. He comes out of nowhere and starts pounding these kids ... he was like a bowling ball knocking down people. And then he picks up one of them—up over his *head*, mind you—and *throws* him at the others."

"Golly," I gasped.

"And those kids just went running away—limping away—like they were being chased by the devil himself," my father said. "And do you know what the strangest part was? Your uncle had this look on his face—all blank and peaceful—and it was like he was hardly there. I had to tell him about tossing the kid ... he didn't even remember."

"Not at all?" I questioned.

"It was like he was in a trance."

"That's amazing," Jack said. "But ... but I thought you said the *two* of you fought five kids."

My father looked embarrassed. "I guess it was really my brother who fought five guys ... but I was there. It just reminded me that what you two did was what brothers should do ... take care of each other."

"Nobody hits my little brother!" Jack snapped. "Well ... except for me."

"That's how it was with my brother, too." He paused. "But I think it's best that we don't tell your mother about that little story."

"We won't," Jack said.

I nodded in agreement.

"Your mother says I should punish you," he said.

He let out a deep breath, like a sigh, as if he was regretting what he was about to say—or do. I figured he wouldn't be the only one regretting it.

"But to tell you the truth ... I'm not sure she's right."

"You aren't?" I said.

"Do *you* think you should be punished?" he asked.

"No!" I exclaimed.

"I don't see how you had much choice. As far as I'm concerned, you didn't do anything except defend yourselves."

"So you'll talk to Mom and explain that—?"

"Oh, no, that won't be happening," he said, cutting Jack off. "In fact, we're going to agree that I gave you a good tongue-lashing and that you both promised this would never happen again."

"It won't," I said.

"Never again," Jack agreed.

"Well … I'm glad you promised." He paused. "But, boys, if anything like this ever *does* happen again—"

"It won't," I said again.

"Let me finish. If you ever need to defend yourselves in the future, you do what you have to do."

"We can fight?" Jack asked.

"Of course you can. Nobody is ever going to use the Braun men for punching bags without getting a few punches back. Now, both of you go and wash up for supper."

"We're getting supper?" I asked hopefully.

"Your mother threatened, but that's one threat she'll never keep. Make sure you wash away any traces of blood, and whatever you do, don't mention being in pain. Understand?"

We nodded our heads in agreement.

He reached out and put a hand on Jack's shoulder and then ruffled my hair.

It was *so* good to have Dad home again.

CHAPTER FIVE

"PASS THE POTATOES," Jack said to me.

"*Please*, pass the potatoes," Mom said.

"*Pleeeeaasse*, pass the potatoes," he said.

I gave him the bowl.

"*Thank you* so much," he said.

"You are *very* welcome. It was *my* pleasure."

"That's *most* kind of you," Jack replied. "You are *such* a gentle—"

"Knock it off or you'll both be back in your room," my father said, interrupting Jack.

"Even pretend manners are better than no manners," my mother said.

"Let's change the subject," my father suggested. "So how was schoo—" He stopped himself mid-sentence as he realized this probably wasn't the best choice of subject.

"*School* was great," I replied. "I have a very nice teacher." Deaf, and not very good—but she was nice.

"I like my class, too," Jack added. "How was your day, Mom?"

"Just the usual routine. You've seen one letter, you've seen them all."

"Some of them must be interesting," my father said.

"We really don't have time to read them," she said. "We're just basically scanning for details around times and places."

My mother was employed as a censor. She went through letters—hundreds and hundreds a day—that were being sent between North America and Europe and Africa. Along with hundreds of other women, her job mainly involved looking at the letters between soldiers and their families, to make sure that nobody was sending information that could help the Nazis if enemy agents obtained it accidentally, or on purpose.

A censor had seen all of the letters we'd received from Dad while he was serving in Africa. Sometimes a word or part of a sentence had been blacked out with a marker, so that we couldn't read what was underneath. I knew Dad wouldn't have said much in those few words, but whatever it was must have revealed something that the censor was worried about.

Now Mom was the censor—one of twelve *hundred*, from what I'd heard. They'd been drawn from Canada, Britain, the United States and other islands besides Bermuda. They all worked in The Princess Hotel, this big pink building down on the bay that had been a real hotel when there were tourists. The Catalina flying boats landed in the harbour. To see them land or take off was amazing. They had big engines, with wheels for landing on regular runways and floats for landing on water. They carried mail between North America and Europe. And all of it, along with the mail carried by ships, was brought over to the hotel by boats, censored and then sent back to continue the journey.

"Have you come across any 'Dear John' letters?" my father asked.

"A few. They're the worst."

"Who's John?" I asked.

My parents both chuckled.

"It's not a person, it's a type of letter," Jack said. "It's a letter to say that somebody doesn't want to be with that person any more ... right?"

"That's right," my father said. "A couple of guys in my regiment got those letters. One was from a girlfriend, but the other one, it was his wife ... she'd met somebody else."

"That is so terrible," my mother said.

"Awful. He's off fighting to save democracy and she gets involved with some *civilian*."

He said "civilian" like it was a dirty word, but I knew what he meant. Most of the men had enlisted, volunteered to defend our country, like my father had, and they didn't have much time for those who weren't willing to fight.

"I can't get over the fact that there are enough letters to keep so many of you occupied," my father said.

"All the letters on the flying boats are routed through Bermuda," my mother explained.

The Atlantic was far too wide for a plane to fly all the way without refuelling, so the flying boats set down in Bermuda.

"That's why we have such strange hours," my mother explained. "When a plane lands, there could be twenty thousand letters and parcels to go through."

"Do you look in the parcels?" I asked.

"Not me," my mother said. "I'm a letter lady."

"But you don't just look at things between soldiers and their families, do you?" Jack asked.

"All communication that goes to and from Europe."

That got my attention. "So you could be reading mail that was sent by spies or enemy agents?"

She didn't answer.

"Sounds like there's a story here," my father said. "Are you reading mail from Mata Hari?"

"'Dear John' I know, but who is that?" Jack asked.

"A famous German spy in World War One who was eventually executed as a double agent," my father said. He turned to my mother. "Well ... have you caught any spies?"

"She can't tell you that," Jack said.

"Official Secrets Act," I added.

"She can't even tell her husband? Wait ... how do you two know about things like the Official Secrets Act?"

I swallowed hard. I knew why I knew about it—after all, we were still sworn to secrecy by it. I couldn't tell my father about any of the things that had happened to us since we'd gotten involved with Camp X. But what was I supposed to tell Dad now?

"*I* told them," my mother lied. "And I'm glad they listened so well."

Wow, she'd said that so *believably*. If I hadn't known any better, I would have believed her. Our mother was really quite the good liar ... something to keep in mind. I mean, if she was so able to tell a convincing lie, could I believe the things she told me or—I stopped myself from going any further in that direction. It was bad enough that I didn't trust anybody outside our home.

"We had two planes land at almost the same time last week," she said. "There were close to forty thousand letters. That was the night I didn't get home until almost midnight."

"I don't like that," my father said.

"Believe me, dear, the boys are fine on their own without me being—"

"It isn't the boys I'm worried about."

She gave him a questioning look.

"I don't like you to be out there late at night," he explained.

"It's not like I'm alone. The downtown is filled with people."

"That's what I don't like," my father said. "All those soldiers, half of them half in the bag. A couple of the Military Police told me it's like a frontier town down there, with drunken brawls in the streets."

"That's mainly Friday and Saturday nights."

"And you sometimes work *those* nights."

"Nobody has ever bothered me."

"And I'd like to keep it that way."

"It's just a bunch of little boys getting into trouble because their mothers and wives and girlfriends aren't here."

"And it's apparently gotten worse since half of those little boys are American soldiers here to build the airfield. They and the British soldiers don't seem to realize that they're allies," my father added.

"What about the Canadians?" my mother asked.

My father shrugged. "I can only speak for *this* Canadian."

"Good, because I think we've had enough fighting from members of this family already."

Wait a minute—somehow this had come back to us again!

"I just wish I could walk you home each night," my father said.

She reached across the table and gave his hands a squeeze. "You're such a sweetie. I'm just glad you're now here instead of halfway around the world."

"I'm glad, too," he said. "Although I still think the whole thing is strange."

"What do you mean?" My mother was trying to sound innocent, but my father was still asking awkward questions about why he had been reassigned, and why we were with him. Apparently the cover story wasn't holding water for him.

"You know what I mean. I'm pulled away from my troops in Africa and reassigned to Bermuda. Doesn't that seem a little bit ... peculiar?"

"I think it's mostly because they needed me here, and since you had to serve somewhere, why not Bermuda? We should just be grateful and not question it too much," my mother said. "Aren't you glad you're here?"

"Of course I am. How could I not be happy about being here with my family instead of being shot at?"

"I guess there's not much chance of being shot here, is there?" I asked.

"Only with a camera," he said. "Although we certainly could do some shooting back if anybody shot at us. They just finished installing the second big eleven-incher at the dockyards."

My father was second-in-command of the guard detail for the dockyards on the far west side of the island—not that anything was that far … it was less than twenty miles away. The British navy for this part of the Atlantic was stationed there, so it was a very important strategic position. My father had told me that sometimes more than two dozen ships were in dock—destroyers, minesweepers, corvettes, frigates and, occasionally, a cruiser or even a full-fledged battleship. Some of the ships became part of convoy duty, providing escorts to protect England-bound ships carrying freight or soldiers from the U-boats. Other ships were part of hunter-killer groups that went looking for the U-boats. That would have been so much better—chasing them instead of running from them.

"Do you think they'll ever have to use those guns?" my mother asked.

"We can only hope not, but we're trying to be prepared for anything."

"Anything … what do you think could happen?" I asked, suddenly feeling a little anxious.

"I doubt there's much chance of a full-fledged invasion."

"That's reassuring," my mother said.

"But there are 138 islands that make up Bermuda."

"That many?" Jack asked.

"And each one has so many inlets and beaches that you couldn't count, let alone patrol or monitor, them all."

"You think somebody could come ashore without being seen?" I asked.

"*Dozens* of people could come ashore without being seen."

"But why would they want to do that?" my mother questioned.

"Espionage and sabotage. The dockyards and the new airfield are prime locations. If I were the enemy, I'd want to know more about them. Take the dockyards. If somebody was in a position to watch ships coming and going from the dockyards, they could radio U-boats ... that could be just offshore, for all we know."

"*Nothing* bad is going to happen," my mother said firmly, in a tone that left no doubt that this conversation was over. "Now, can I get anybody anything else to eat?"

"Are there any more carrots?" my father asked.

"I think there are a few more in the pot on the stove."

"I'll go and—"

"No, stay here," my mother said as she got to her feet and went to the kitchen.

"She's right," my father said. "There's nothing to worry about. Well ... I still worry about your mother when I'm not here. "

"We'll help take care of her," Jack said.

"I know you will. You two seem so grown up. I was gone less than two years and you two have grown from boys to men."

"I know *I* have," Jack said and then pointed at me. "But him?"

"Well, a *young* man, at least. I'm just grateful you're both around to keep an eye on things. You know I count on you two boys—"

"Hey, what happened to 'young men'?" Jack said.

"Right, I meant you two young *men*—I count on you to watch out for your mother when I can't be here."

I caught Jack's eye—it sounded as though we'd been given a new mission!

CHAPTER SIX

"GOOD PRACTICE, MATES!" Trevor said as he shook hands with Jack and then slapped me on the back.

I tried not to wince in pain. "Thanks. You too."

We walked away from the change room, leaving our new teammates behind. I looked over at Jack. His face was covered in mud but a smile peeked through.

"How are you feeling?" I asked.

"A little sore, but I'm not sure how much of that is from the fight and how much is from the practice. Rugby is one rough game."

"Yeah. I was wondering if they invited us to join the team just so they could keep on hitting us."

Jack laughed. "That thought crossed my mind, too."

"Do you understand much of the rules?"

"The basic ones. Louise was explaining them to me at lunch."

"That's only fair because, if you think about it, she's the reason we're on the team," I joked.

"I think you're right. And she's really ... different."

"She *is* English."

"It's not just that. She's been to a lot of different places and done some interesting things," Jack said.

"Probably not *nearly* as interesting as the things you've done," I said. "Not that you can tell her about any of it."

"I think I know that," Jack snapped. "But she's travelled so much. She's been all through Europe, you know, before the war."

"Yeah, but has she been to Whitby, or Bowmanville, or—"

"I don't think she's even heard of those places. She was telling me about Rome and how beautiful Paris is in the spring and—"

"Sounds like she's bragging," I said, cutting him off.

"No, not bragging ... she's not like that."

"I haven't really talked to her. Maybe you should invite her to dinner."

Jack laughed. "Yeah, right."

"Why not? It's a guarantee that Mom will like her."

He gave me a questioning look.

"Assuming she's not a Nazi spy, she's already way ahead of your last girlfriend."

I regretted those words—again—even before Jack punched me in the arm.

"It's nice of you boys to walk me down to the train," our father said.

"We thought we could then go and meet Mom at work and walk her home."

Dad didn't say anything, but he gave a little smile to let us know he approved of what we were doing.

The walk from our house toward the town was downhill. Stretched out in front of us were the town of Hamilton and the harbour beyond that. It was a beautiful scene, pastel-coloured buildings against the emerald green of the water. It was so different from Ajax or Whitby, or anywhere I'd ever lived or been or even seen in pictures. It was sort of like living in a postcard from some exotic place. We *were* living in an exotic place—on a tropical island. Who would have thought that our adventures would lead us to Bermuda?

Hamilton wasn't very big, but our teacher had told us it was a lot bigger than before the war. Then, it had been a sleepy little town visited only by tourists who came in by ship. Now the tourists were all gone, replaced by the soldiers and sailors who had flooded onto the island. Hotels that used to be filled with tourists had either closed down or been taken over by the military, like The Princess, where my mother worked.

We followed Wesley Street toward the water. Off to our left stood the big cathedral. Its steeple, soaring over everything, was the tallest structure on the island. Or maybe the lighthouse up on Gibbs Hill was taller. We lived close enough to both to hear the cathedral bells chiming on Sunday morning and to see the sweep of the light from the top of the lighthouse when it was turned on. The lighthouse was used only when they knew a plane or ship was due to arrive. Otherwise it was dark, like the rest of the island. All the houses and businesses turned off their lights at night, or used blackout shades so light wouldn't leak out. No sense in giving enemy ships or planes handy points of navigation. Better that they find themselves wrecked on the reefs and rocks in the waters that surrounded the island.

The lighthouse was off limits to non-military personnel, but Jack and I had talked about going to the top of the cathedral so we could see the view from up there. I was always a little nervous of heights but it would be worth it—to see a postcard view from a postcard viewpoint. Bermuda really was beautiful.

We turned onto Front Street. It was alive with activity. There were dozens and dozens of horses and carriages, slowly moving down the wide dirt roadway or tied up in front of the stores and hotels. Right down the middle of the road ran the railroad tracks that linked one end of the island to the other. We'd only been on the train once, for a short run. I hoped someday we could go the whole way to the end, out at the dockyards, to see our father.

"There's the train," my father said. "We better do double time." We started to move more quickly.

The train was slowly coming through town. As it rolled forward, it clanged its bell to move people and horses off the tracks. It was a very small train. In fact, even calling it a train was kind of generous. It was three cars long and looked more like the streetcars we'd seen in Toronto. We got to the station, and my father joined the end of the line waiting to board.

"I wonder who had the bright idea to put a train right in the middle of the road," Jack said.

"Probably wasn't much of a problem before they had cars," I commented.

"Not that they have many now, but I still can't believe that they *just* allowed cars in Bermuda."

Almost on cue a big army truck came rolling slowly down the street, as people and horses scurried out of the way.

"People here say that's the biggest change the war has brought," our father said. "Even now, vehicles are only supposed to be used for military purposes."

The big army truck lumbered past us, and we could see that the back was filled with American soldiers. The

Americans dominated the whole east side of the island, where they were building an airport. I hadn't actually seen it but I'd heard all about it. They were using gigantic machines to dredge mud from the bay, which they dumped to make the island bigger so that it could accommodate two long runways. They were also building a bridge— well, more like a causeway—to link the airfield to the main island. Maybe one day Jack and I would go out there to see what they were doing.

"Okay, boys, I'll see you in a week," our father said. "Take care of things," he added.

"Yes, sir," Jack replied.

He shook our hands. We were too old to be hugged— especially in public.

The train glided into the station and came to a stop. People got off through the back doors of the cars as those waiting in line boarded through the front doors. There were some soldiers getting on but it was mainly local people. The train was the very best way for anybody to get from one end of the island to the other. The soldiers some- times had the choice of a military vehicle. The locals could also walk, ride a bike or take a horse and carriage, but the train was a lot faster than any of those.

We stood and watched as Dad climbed on. We lost sight of him for an instant and then he reappeared, leaned down, looked through one of the windows and waved to us. We waved back and the train started away, clanging its bell again to clear a path. How strange—how wonderful—to know that he wasn't going far, and that he'd be back in seven days ... and nobody was going to be trying to kill him.

"What time is it now?" Jack asked.

I looked at my watch. "Almost four-thirty."

"Just about perfect timing," Jack said. "Mom will be getting off work at five."

We walked along Front Street toward the hotel. The street was full of activity. Horses and carriages jockeyed with military trucks, the occasional car and throngs of pedestrians. We stayed off to the side of the road. I kept one eye on the harbour as we walked. There were two big ships and a few smaller ones tied up to the pier, and dozens of little motor skiffs and sailboats out on the water. This was supposed to be a "safe" waterway because the narrow entrance from the ocean was blocked by a submarine net and protected by artillery battalions on both sides.

I thought more about what my father had said at dinner about the possibility of U-boats being just offshore. I knew what he was saying was true. A U-boat in the middle of the night could certainly come in undetected, so close that a few men could launch a rubber dinghy that would make its way to shore. Put those agents in civilian clothes, or an

TROUBLE IN PARADISE   55

Allied soldier's or sailor's uniform, and they could pretty well go anywhere they wanted.

I looked at the people around us. Any one of them could be an enemy agent. Maybe that man, or that woman pushing the stroller ... was there even a baby in there? Or that sailor ... he did have very blond hair and— I stopped myself. I couldn't allow my thoughts to go down that road.

"There's the hotel," Jack said.

"It looks like a wedding cake to me," I said.

"A pink wedding cake?"

"You know what I mean."

The hotel was pink—pastel coloured, like every other building on the island—topped with the obligatory white limestone roof to capture rainwater. It was four storeys tall, very long and just about the largest building on the island.

In front of the hotel, where there probably used to be manicured lawns and flower beds, there were sentries, a guard house, barbed wire and two machine gun nests protected by sandbags. I wondered what the tourists who used to frequent this hotel would have thought of all this.

"Let's go and sit down over there," Jack said.

We crossed the street, again watching for vehicles. There weren't many, but we had to be careful because they were driving on the wrong side of the road ... well, wrong for us, the left-hand side, like in England. That still confused me. We slumped to the ground, shaded by a low wall, some bushes and a tall palm tree. I looked up into the branches of the palm—no coconuts. I'd heard about people being bonked by falling coconuts. After all I'd been through, I wasn't going to cash in my chips that way.

When I shifted, the pain in my ribs made me yelp ever so slightly.

Jack chuckled.

"Sure, like *you're* not feeling any pain anywhere."

"I'm not complaining," Jack said.

"Your face must really be hurting."

"It's not that—"

"'Cause it's hurting *me* just to look at it."

"Brave words from somebody who knows his mommy is close at hand to save him," Jack said.

"You know, you're not *that* much stronger than me," I said as I tried to sit taller.

"Do you really want to go down that road?" Jack asked, with a hint of menace in his voice.

"Ummm ... not really. Look, people are starting to come out."

Two women, followed by a group of four, came out past the sentries.

"And we're not the only ones waiting to meet some-body," I said. There was a group of soldiers and sailors waiting directly in front of the hotel.

"Maybe just hoping to meet somebody," Jack said.

"What do you …? Oh, never mind … I get it."

The women walked past the men, who tried to strike up conversations with them. The women kept walking and the men stayed back as more women came out.

"Only makes sense," Jack said. "Thousands of men stationed on the island and hundreds of women working at the hotel. Like bees to honey."

"One of those *honeys* is our mother," I pointed out. "I don't like that at all—"

I tried to get to my feet but Jack reached out and pulled me back down. He was still a lot stronger than me.

"Don't be a little goof. Mom can take care of herself. Besides, they're not after old married ladies."

"Wait till I tell Mom you called her old."

"Better keep your mouth shut or you won't live long enough to grow old," Jack threatened. "There's Mom now … watch."

Mom walked out with three other ladies. They all seemed older than most of the others. Together they walked through the gauntlet of soldiers and sailors. Some of the men tipped their hats or appeared to say something, but the ladies just walked through and were left alone. They turned up Front Street, walking away from us.

"See, she's okay," Jack said.

He started to get up but I pulled him back down.

"What are you doing?" he demanded.

"She hasn't seen us," I said. "Let's tail her."

"Why would we do that?"

"To make sure that nobody does bother her. If we're beside her, we won't know for sure if people really leave her alone." I paused. "Besides, it might be fun."

"I can think of better ways to have fun," Jack said.

"Okay, so we'll do it just to see if we can. Come on."

Jack shrugged. "Why not?"

We both got to our feet, but we waited. We wanted to let her get farther ahead. She continued to walk with the other women along the edge of the far side of the road. We watched, but we didn't move until there were lots of people and passing carriages between our mom and us. Then we started after her.

She was chatting with the other women, not looking back, not even looking around. So far, this was a piece of cake. Continuing along Front Street, the crowds of pedestrians and the traffic got heavier. That made it easier for us to find cover. But then she looked to the right, and the left—almost straight at us—and crossed the street. We froze in place. She hadn't seen us, but she certainly *could* have. Now she was on our side of the street, and there really wasn't any place to hide.

Jack grabbed my hand and dragged me up a side street. We were out of sight—but so was she.

"Come on," Jack said. "We'll go this way."

"But she's going along—"

"She's only going along Front for another block and then she's going to cut up Queen Street."

"Oh, yeah, that's right. I guess it's easier to follow somebody when you already know where they're going."

"We'll get back on her tail by cutting across the park. We won't lose her for long."

Jack and I started running. It was uphill, away from the harbour. We cut between two stores, along an alley and then into a park. There were paths, but we went across the grass and between the trees. We crossed partway and then Jack came to a stop behind a big cedar tree.

"We'll be able to see her from here as she passes," he said.

The words had hardly left his mouth when she did pass by—going up Queen. We waited a few seconds until the post office blocked her from view.

We ran to the building and Jack peered around and up the street. I bent down so I could see, too. She was a few storefronts ahead of us.

"We'll wait here until she gets farther ... at least a dozen or so stores."

That made sense.

"Okay, just wait another ... Now! Let's go now!" Jack said.

We started out after her. She was quite a long way up the road, but there were very few people between us. If she glanced backward, we'd be seen for sure.

"Let's cross to the other side," I suggested.

Four horses, pulling a milk cart, were coming up the road. We let them pass and then fell in behind. Good cover. The cart was moving up the hill at a faster pace than we normally would have walked, so we had to jog to keep up. It was perfect cover, but we couldn't stay with it for very long because we were gaining on our mother. We circled around to the side of the cart, keeping it between her and us, and then moved off to the sidewalk.

The milk wagon continued to move forward—it was still blocking our view of Mom ... wasn't it?

"Where is she now?" Jack asked.

She was nowhere to be seen. I looked up and down the street—it was like she'd vanished into thin air! Had she been kidnapped or—?

"The bakery," Jack said. "She's gone into the bakery ... look through the window."

I squinted slightly, peering through the glare of the glass. Of course that was where she'd gone. Mom often brought home fresh buns and bread when she came from work. Sometimes she'd even bring a couple of jelly-filled donuts. I loved those donuts.

"Hide," Jack said.

We bumped together as we both tried to fit behind a slender tree. It didn't hide us completely, but enough so that she couldn't tell it was us. I peeked around the tree as she came out of the bakery, carrying a bag, and turned back along her route toward home.

Jack and I shuffled around, keeping the tree between her and us as she crossed Church Street and continued up the hill on Wesley. We trailed along, block by block, at a very safe distance, making sure that we kept her in sight. Our street was just up ahead and she'd soon make the turn. We'd done it. We'd followed her the whole way without being seen!

"What are we going to say when she asks where we were?" Jack asked. "It's not like we can tell her we were tailing her."

"Well, we could tell her that we walked Dad to the train."

"And then she'll want to know why we didn't go and meet her. Where did we go after we said goodbye to Dad?"

"I hadn't thought of that," I admitted.

Mom made the turn onto our street and disappeared. "Maybe we don't have to tell her anything," Jack said with a grin. "Come on!"

He started running and turned onto the street *before* our street. He was moving fast and I had to work hard to keep up with him. My legs were sore—rugby-practice sore—but I couldn't complain or ask him to slow down.

Suddenly he turned into the driveway of a house— What was he doing? I took off after him as he ran along the side of the house and— There was *our* house on the other side of a low concrete wall!

Jack didn't even slow down. He jumped over the wall, putting one hand on top to propel himself. It was higher than it looked and I had to scramble over, climbing more than jumping.

The back door of the house was unlocked and we ran inside, quickly kicking off our shoes and settling in at the kitchen table, where our homework was already waiting for us.

"Pretty slick," I huffed as I struggled to catch my breath.

Jack smirked and I thought he was going to say something ... when we heard the front door open.

"Hello!" Mom called out.

"We're in the kitchen!" Jack called back. "We're doing our homework!"

She came into the room. "I have to see this first-hand." She gave us each a kiss on the top of the head.

"Just trying to be conscientious students," Jack said.

Mom laughed. "Very nice to see. You look like you've been working far too hard."

We looked at her questioningly.

"You're both sweating, and it isn't even that hot in here," she said.

"We were sort of roughhousing a little bit," I said.

"But we have been working hard," Jack added. "Maybe so hard that we deserve a reward. Could we have a jelly donut before supper?"

"I think that might be … wait a minute, how did you know that I bought jelly donuts?"

I looked at Mom. She wasn't carrying the bag—she must have left it at the front door. How could we possibly explain?

"Isn't it obvious?" I asked. "The smell … I can smell fresh bread. Can't you, Jack? Mom must have gone to the bakery … and she wouldn't go to the bakery without buying her beloved sons their favourite donuts. Would you, Mom?"

"Of course she wouldn't!" Jack added. "So … are there jelly donuts?"

She laughed. "Two donuts coming up for my hard-working boys."

CHAPTER SEVEN

I LOOKED UP into the night through branches and leaves. There had to be a million stars. The combination of a clear, cloudless sky and the almost total darkness because of the blackout rules made them all visible. The moon was a sliver of brilliant white light, but it wasn't bright enough to distract from or hide the stars.

I took a deep breath. It was clean sea air, but cool. I was glad I was wearing a sweater, but it was more the colour than the cold that had caused me to put it on. The sweater was black. Like my pants and my socks. The only things that weren't black were my shoes, and the dirt I'd rubbed into them had helped to erase any traces of white canvas.

"Do you see anything?" Jack called up from the lower branches of the tree in which we both sat.

"Nothing," I replied. I could see lots of things but I knew what he meant. Did I see our mother or anybody else coming out of the hotel?

It couldn't be much longer. At least, I *hoped* it couldn't be. We'd been sitting in the tree for almost two hours. It was a great place to see and not be seen. Who looked for people up in a tree at night?

I held on to a branch with one hand and looked at my watch to check the time. I turned my wrist back and forth, trying to catch enough light to see the hands. No luck. It had to be at least eleven. I was just grateful that Mom was working so late on a Saturday and not a school night, or we wouldn't have been able to stay out and watch over her.

We'd followed her home three times already over the last two weeks. We obviously couldn't do it every night, but when we could, we did. It was what Dad wanted, it was keeping her safe, and it was exciting—not just trailing her, but being out and downtown, especially on a night like this.

The blackout rules might have dimmed the city lights, but apparently that didn't stop people from going out on a Saturday night. We were at least two blocks away from the nearest hotel down the way on Front Street, but I could still hear voices—talking, arguing, yelling and even singing ... badly. The downtown strip was crowded with hundreds of soldiers and sailors. It was obvious that more than a few of them had had something to drink—maybe a *lot* of something to drink. Among the military personnel were the M.P.s—Military Police—who were there to keep order. From what I'd been told, that was a losing battle. It was just a matter of time before a fight started. It could be between sailors and soldiers, or Americans and Brits, or the locals and the soldiers or maybe even between two best buddies who had drunk too much. Once started, a lot of them turned into full-fledged brawls. That made us even gladder that we were here to watch out for our mom.

My eye caught a movement at the sentry gate in front of the hotel.

"Can you see who it is?" Jack asked. Obviously he had seen something, too.

"I can't see much … one person … maybe a man …"

A dark figure came from behind the sandbags. It obviously wasn't Mom. It was a man … a little man, a little *old* man. He turned and headed in our direction, away from the downtown. He moved slowly, more shuffling than walking, and he was bent over as if the satchel he carried was weighing him down. He wore a long, dark trench coat, all buttoned up, and had a large fedora on his head, the rim throwing shadows so that it was impossible to see his features.

I felt myself tensing, holding my breath, as he went by. I looked down, past Jack, to the road below, only able to see the top of his head as he passed directly beneath us. He continued shuffling down the road, moving painfully slowly. So why was an old geezer coming out of The Princess ... especially this late at night?

He was almost lost from sight when a dark shape stepped out from an alleyway and started in the same direction.

"Did you see that?" Jack asked.

I nodded my head and then realized he couldn't see a nod. "Yeah, I saw."

"Look how slowly he's moving," Jack said. "The same speed as the old guy."

"Do you think he's trailing him?" I asked.

"Could just be a coincidence."

The instant Jack said that, I knew we were thinking the same thing—a good spy didn't believe in coincidences.

"Do you think we should do something?" I asked, realizing that there was only one thing we could do.

Without another word we both started to climb down from the tree, trying not to make any noise. By the time we reached the ground, the old man was lost in the darkness, but we could still see the man who was following him.

We moved silently on our sneaker-clad feet along the grassy patch that paralleled the road. From our dark clothes, to our shoes, to the distance and the angle of our pursuit, we'd been working on our technique. It wasn't only our mother we'd been trailing—we'd followed other people, too. We were playing a game—and we'd become better at it.

My feet were silent but my heart was pounding as we kept pace, not moving too fast. We didn't want to catch up with the second man, or with the old guy ahead of him. Our subject turned down an alleyway leading toward the ocean.

We hurried to the entrance and then stopped. Carefully, we both looked around the corner of the building. The narrow alley was pitch-black. I couldn't see anything beyond a couple of dozen yards. And the man we were following had vanished into the darkness.

"What now?" I whispered.

"We have to be careful."

That sounded like a good plan. We could find a spot outside the alley and keep watch, or maybe find another way around without going down the alley, or—

"Let's go," Jack said.

As he started to move into the alley, I grabbed his arm. "You said we were going to be careful," I hissed.

"We are. We're going to move *carefully* down the alley. Be quiet and stay behind me."

He brushed off my hand and began creeping forward. Against my better judgment, I followed.

It was definitely darker and we couldn't move very quickly. That was good. Slow was quiet. Slow meant that the guy we were following was getting farther ahead. Losing him was a problem, but catching up to him would have been a bigger one. As we walked, I kept my hand against the wall as a guide.

The alley ended, opening up to a courtyard. Beyond that was the ocean. With no overhang from the buildings, the courtyard seemed almost bright. The stars provided enough illumination so I could see the entire area. There were buildings on two sides ... was one of them a stable? There were a couple of carriages and some farm equipment ... some rowboats on their sides by the water ... but no people.

"Jack, do you—?"

He put a hand on my mouth to silence me, and gestured to the far end of the courtyard. There, in the shadows, I saw movement. It was a man— Was it the man we were following? He was pressed against the side of the building, and it looked as though he was trying to peer through a window. Was that where the old man had gone? Was he in that building?

Almost in answer to my questions, the door opened and the old man appeared. He walked slowly, and he no longer carried the satchel. Had he left it in the building? What if he wanted to come back this way? We were right in the alley—there was no way he could pass without seeing us.

"Hands up!" yelled a voice.

Suddenly men rushed out of that building and ran across the courtyard, flashlights flaring, the beams converging on the man we'd been following who was hiding by the side of the building. With one hand he shielded his eyes—and a gun was in his other hand! There was a flash from the gun and a shot rang out … and then there was gunfire from everywhere. The man was hit repeatedly and sprawled forward, collapsing to the ground, the whole show captured in the beams of the flashlights!

CHAPTER EIGHT

I GASPED and went weak in the knees. My legs almost buckled under me. Jack grabbed my arm to steady me, and then I staggered forward as he half-dragged me down the alley. We slipped into the darkness, Jack still holding on to me and—

"Stop right there!" a voice called out. "You in the alley, stop! Now!"

I hesitated slightly but Jack's strong hand kept pulling me forward, and then beams of light came bouncing up the alleyway, hitting the walls and ground!

"Run!" Jack screamed. I didn't need any encouragement. I was keeping up with him, step for step and— Lights appeared at the end of the alley. We skidded to a stop. Two dark figures holding flashlights were blocking our way out! The beams of their lights came toward us. Behind us were loud footsteps, echoing off the walls, filling my ears. We were trapped!

"Stay where you are. Hands up, or we'll shoot!" shouted a voice from behind.

I started to raise my hands but Jack grabbed me by the arm and nearly pulled me off my feet. "This way!"

I stumbled forward and a bullet whizzed past our heads! I jumped in shock and then staggered sideways, falling to my knees, but Jack's grip hauled me back to my feet and we almost fell into a little walkway running off the alley. Jack was still dragging me along as we ran down the passage.

"In here," Jack said, and we tripped through a doorway, landing on the wooden floor.

"Go over there," Jack whispered. "Hide in the corner."

I crawled until I banged into a wall, then turned. Jack had run to a door at the other side of the building. He threw it open. He was leaving me! Wait, he couldn't leave me here ... for them! Then he ran back across the room and practically threw himself on top of me, pinning me to the ground. I let out a tiny gasp.

"Shut up!" he whispered. "Not a sound."

No sooner were the words out of his mouth than the door we'd entered through was kicked in with a thunderous smash and the sound of splintering wood. Flashlight beams preceded the men—two, then another and another and another—and they were all holding guns.

"They've gone out this way!" one of the men screamed.

The men rushed to the other door, beams of light bouncing and their bodies bumping together as they scrambled out.

That was why Jack had opened the door! That was genius!

"Jack, that was——"

He put a hand over my mouth. So much for my compliments.

Two more flashlight beams entered through the first door, then another. One of the beams played around the room, searching. If it fell on us, we'd be caught.

"The door. They've all gone that way!"

Three more lights followed by three more men went out the second door, leaving us alone again.

"We have to get out of here," Jack said. He started to get up, but I held him back.

"No. We have to stay still. They didn't see us."

"They didn't see us the *first* time, but when they can't find us out there, they'll double back and really search."

Unfortunately, what he said made sense. They would be coming back.

"Maybe we can hide better," I suggested.

"That won't work. As soon as they realize that they last saw us running in here, they'll tear this place apart ... and us, too, once they find us."

Again, that made sense. We had to leave.

Jack got up and started for the door through which they had all just left. I grabbed him again, and he knocked my grip from his sweater.

"We have no choice," he hissed. "We have to leave."

"I know, but we can't leave through the door they went out," I said. "If they do double back, we'll walk right into them. We have to double back as well. We have to use the door we came in through."

Jack didn't answer, but he headed straight for it and I fell in behind him. He stopped at the darkened door, smashed and hanging ajar. Too bad there wasn't more light because then we could have seen if anybody was … no, wait … if anybody was out there, we'd see their flashlights. Those beams of light could help them see us, but it worked both ways.

Jack was still standing at the door, cautiously trying to look out, when I brushed past him and stepped into the alley. He was right on my heels. He tapped me on the shoulder and pointed back the way we'd originally walked, away from where most of the men had gathered, away from where the shooting had taken place. I didn't need to be told twice which way to go.

We moved silently up the alley, retracing our steps. I tried to look ahead and listen behind, straining for traces of footfalls, voices, beams of light or a bullet being fired. I heard nothing except the very, very quiet sound of our sneakers against the cobblestones.

We reached the end of the alley, but instead of being safer, we were suddenly in even more danger. By stepping out of the shadows cast by the buildings to where there was more light, we were more visible. Jack took off to the left, away from downtown in the opposite direction from which we had come, and from which those men had exited the building.

We crossed the road and the sound of our shoes on the gravel seemed deafening. Soon enough, though, we hit the grass and soil on the other side and then ran headlong into a stand of trees. We kept moving at a good clip, and with each step the canopy of the trees produced more cover, more shadow, until I could hardly make out Jack a few feet in front of me.

Jack slowed down a bit, and then a bit more until he finally came to a stop. He slumped on the ground, his back against a tree, and I took a seat almost on top of him.

"Do you think—?"

"Shut up," he hissed. "Just listen."

I turned my head, aiming one ear back the way we'd come. Nothing. Slowly I rotated my head, trying to pick up any sounds. Except for the singing of the tree frogs, there was nothing—well, nothing except the sound of our own heavy breathing. And the pounding of my heart pulsing in my ears, but I knew that couldn't be heard by anybody else.

"Do you think we lost——?"

"Keep your voice down," he whispered.

"Sorry. Do you think we lost them?"

"I hope so."

"Then maybe we should get going, get farther away."

"Just sit ... catch your breath ... if we don't make noise and don't move, they won't be able to find us."

"But we can't sit here all night."

"We can sit here for another hour or so," he whispered.

"But what will Mom say if she gets home and we're not there?" I asked.

"I think she'd rather we be late than dead." He chuckled. "I can't believe you're more afraid of Mom than some men with guns."

"I can't believe you *aren't*."

Jack almost laughed but stopped himself.

We stayed where we were and I worked hard at trying to slow down my heartbeat, control my breathing. I knew it would be better to be calm and rested if we needed to run again. I tried not to think about what had just happened ... what *had* happened? No, I couldn't think of that yet, so I tried to just listen to the tree frogs and concentrate on slowing my heart and my breathing.

I looked up through the canopy of branches. Twinkling stars were still visible among the leaves. Suddenly I felt tired, very tired. If I closed my eyes, I could almost drift off, right here and now.

"Time to go," Jack said. He started off through the trees, and I quickly fell in behind him.

"Where are we going?"

"Home, of course."

"But ... but ... isn't home that way?" I asked, pointing in a direction almost opposite to the way we were heading.

"It is, but we're not going straight there. We'll make a big circle and come around to it from the far side."

"We can do that? You know where you're going?"

"I can try. Besides, it's a little island. How lost could I get?"

I wasn't going to argue, even though we both knew it wasn't really that small an island and we could get lost really easily. It was still a good idea. Silently we moved through the stand of trees and came out to a narrow dirt path. I thought we were going to follow it, but Jack cut right across, leading us up the driveway of a small house.

"Do you know who lives here?" I asked.

"We're not visiting. I just want to stay in the brush and off the paths."

There was no light coming from the house. Either they weren't home, or they'd gone to bed or they had incredibly tight blackout screens. We passed by, not hearing any sounds, not making any sounds. Behind the house were more trees and then a slight hill leading down to a dry creek bed. With no trees overtop, the stars were bright enough to guide our way.

"What do you think happened back there?" I asked.

"Seems pretty simple. Somebody was shot and killed ... weren't you watching?"

"I know somebody was shot. That isn't what I meant. Why was he shot? Who shot him, and what do we do about it?"

"In answer to your three questions—I don't know, and I don't know, and I guess I don't know."

"But we have to *do* something."

"We *are* doing something," he said. "We're trying to get away."

"I mean after that. We have to tell somebody," I said.

We broke through some bushes and found ourselves in a field, looking up at the lighthouse. I had no idea we'd travelled this far, but at least we now knew where we were and how to get back home—though we had a long way to go yet.

"So you still haven't answered my question. Who are we going to tell?" I asked again.

"I wish we could tell Bill or Little Bill."

"Me too. They'd know exactly what to do," I agreed. "But we don't even know how to get in touch with them, and they're thousands of miles away."

"Then I guess we're going to have to tell Mom," Jack replied.

I didn't like that, but what other choice did we have?

"Besides, we're going to have to tell her something when we walk in and she asks us where we've been," Jack said.

"Oh, yeah … I'd sort of forgotten about that."

All this time I'd thought that getting home would mean that we'd be safe. Now I wasn't so sure.

My feet were sore, my legs were tired and my hands and face were burning from branches that had whacked against me. But I felt good. There was our house—and better yet, I couldn't see any traces of light leaking out from behind the blackout screens. Mom wasn't home yet.

"We did it. Mom hasn't gotten home," I said.

"Unless she's home and asleep," Jack suggested.

"There's no way if she found the house empty that she'd just go to sleep."

"What if she thought we were in bed and already asleep so she went to bed herself?" Jack asked.

"Well … well … let's go in through the back door," I suggested. "Really quietly."

We circled around the house. There was no hint of light and no sounds. Jack put his hand on the doorknob and turned it. The door opened silently.

"We're good," Jack said.

"Ssshhhhh!"

"She's not home."

"How can you be so—?"

"The door is unlocked. If she was home, she would have locked the door, right?"

He was right. She locked down everything before heading to bed.

Jack turned on the kitchen light. "What time is it?" he asked.

I looked at my watch. "Twelve-thirty. We'd better get to bed ... Mom won't be that much longer."

"Yeah, right," Jack agreed.

We walked into the living room and—

"Good evening, gentlemen."

I skidded to a stop, shocked. There was someone sitting in the wingback chair, the glow of a cigarette lighting his shadowy figure.

CHAPTER NINE

"WHO ... WHO ARE YOU?" Jack said, his voice breaking over the last word.

"Who *I* am is not important," he said. "Where you are going is much more important."

"We're not going anywhere," Jack said, a defiant tone coming into his voice.

"There is an important difference between brave words and foolish actions," the man said. He spoke with an accent, but it wasn't German ... was it? "And do not even think about trying to escape," he added.

That was exactly what I was thinking about. I turned slightly toward Jack, looking for a signal. What were we going to do? When were we going to run?

My attention was caught by movement off to the side. I turned. There was a man standing at the entrance to our bedroom. I realized then that two more men stood behind

us in the kitchen doorway. Nobody had any weapons—
at least I didn't see any guns—but they had every exit
blocked, and we were outnumbered and out-muscled.

"Who are you?" Jack demanded.

"We are not here to answer your questions," the man
said. "You will—"

Jack leaped toward the man, but he got no more than
a couple of steps before he was tackled from behind and
knocked to the floor, pinned under the weight of two
men! I jumped backward and was grabbed, a thick arm
locked under my neck and both my hands held in place so
I couldn't move.

"There is no point in trying to escape," the man said.

"You'll see the point when I pound you out!" Jack
screamed.

"You are in no position to make threats," the man said.

"It's no threat, it's a promise! As soon as I get these gor-
illas off my back, I'm going to make sure you never forget
the beating I give you!"

The man chuckled, and I could see slight smiles on the
faces of some of the other men. They weren't taking his
threat very seriously while he was locked beneath their
weight and muscle. I figured we had to try to bluff our way
out of this, give them something else to think or worry
about. For starters, we had to change the numbers, get rid
of some of them so we at least had a chance.

"You think we came alone?" I said. "Right now this *whole* house is *surrounded*."

I hoped that might make two or three of them go outside to check.

"Yes, it is surrounded," the man replied calmly.

That was not the reaction I'd hoped for.

"It is surrounded by more operatives—*our* agents. Now, you can choose to come with us quietly, or if not, we could gag you and tie you up. Which do you prefer?"

"We're not going to make it any easier for you to—"

"Yes, we'll go along the easy way!" I snapped, cutting Jack off.

He flashed angry eyes at me. I didn't care. Untied, we'd have a better chance of escaping.

"We'll co-operate," I said. "But first, where are you taking us?"

"To see your mother."

"Our mother!" Jack said. "If you've harmed her in any way, I swear I'll kill you!" he growled.

"Again, you are in no position to—"

Somehow Jack got an arm free and punched one of the men on top of him in the face. The man screamed in pain and blood exploded from his nose. Another man jumped on top of Jack, wrestling him back into submission.

"Tie him up!" the leader screamed. "Tie them *both* up!"

Before I could move, I was spun around and a loop of rope was slipped over my wrists. I tried my best to struggle free but it was impossible.

"George, please, do not make this any harder on yourself," one of the men said.

George …? "How do you know my name?"

"We know many things. Just stay calm. Everything will be fine. Trust us."

"Yeah!" Jack screamed out. "We always trust people who knock us down and tie us up!"

He was fighting back so violently that he was making it hard for four men to hold him in place.

"Enough," the leader said.

Like magic, a pistol suddenly appeared in his hand. He held it directly in front of Jack's face.

"You will not resist any more."

Jack stopped fighting.

"We will go out to the waiting vehicle. You will both walk without making a sound. If you cause us any more distress, you will, shall we say, deeply regret your decision. Understand?"

I nodded my head. Jack didn't answer but he didn't argue, which was as close as he was going to get to agreeing.

With our hands bound behind our backs and a man holding us on each side, we were walked out. In front of our house was a large truck. It was black and its headlights were turned off. They led us to the back, where a tarp was removed and the tailgate was lowered with a loud thud. They lifted and passed us like a bag of potatoes from one set of powerful hands to another into the back of the truck. The four men who held us climbed in, joining two others, along with us.

Right away the tailgate was lifted and the tarp tied down, blocking the light and our only way out. They plopped me on a bench on one side of the truck and sat Jack opposite me. We both had a man on each side of us. There was the metallic sound of doors closing and then the truck lurched forward, throwing me toward the back and into one of the men. I tried to push myself upright, but not being able to use my hands made me pretty helpless.

"Where are we going?" I asked.

"You'll find out soon enough," one of the men said. He also had an accent, but different from the leader's.

The truck made a sharp turn and I could feel that we were heading down a hill, toward the downtown. That wasn't what I had expected. Somehow I'd thought they'd take us someplace deserted. Then again, none of the people on the street could see us inside, and it wasn't like we could call out to get their attention.

"How's your nose?" Jack asked.

For a split second I thought he was talking to me before I remembered the blow he'd gotten in.

"I've taken harder punches," the man beside me replied.

"Being punched harder isn't much to brag about," Jack said. "But once I'm out of these ropes, I'll see if I can do a bit better."

"You're lucky you're tied up," the man threatened.

"Me? You're the one who's too afraid even to sit beside me!" Jack taunted. "Big, strong, brave man is afraid of a boy half his age who's—"

"It's you who should be afraid of me!" the man snapped. He jumped to his feet, and the truck lurched to one side. That's when I reached out and kicked him in the back of the leg with all my might! When he tumbled forward, Jack jumped to his feet, and before two of the men could restrain him, he smashed the top of his head into the man's face. The big guy screamed in pain and toppled to the floor. Two of the men grabbed Jack and two others grabbed me, and all of us, in one big mass, landed on top of the big guy!

I started to scream as loudly as I could, hoping to attract the attention of somebody on the street, but a hand was shoved against my mouth. I shook my head violently and the hand moved away slightly, and then a finger slipped into my mouth and I bit down as hard as I could! The owner of the hand screamed in pain and thrashed about desperately as he tried to remove his finger, but I dug my teeth in deeper and deeper. And then I was smashed in the face! I think I actually bit down harder for an instant before my mouth popped open and I released the finger.

Crushed under the weight of bodies, I was finding it hard even to draw a breath. Suddenly we all shifted forward as the truck came to an abrupt stop, the brakes squealing loudly. I heard the sounds of people rushing around outside the truck and then the tarp was pulled back, letting in more light, and the tailgate opened. I was roughly hauled to my feet by two men, one holding each arm, and dragged to the edge of the truck and— My mouth opened in shock. This was the last thing—the last *person*—I'd expected to see.

Standing there, expressionless, his arms folded, was Little Bill. And beside him was our mother.

CHAPTER TEN

"HERE IS YOUR TEA," Little Bill said as he handed me the cup.

I held it with two hands to try to stop from shaking—or at least from letting anybody know that I was shaking. We were sitting in the dining room of The Princess Hotel. There were dozens of tables in the big fancy room. It was beautiful, and empty, except for the four of us.

"Is it not to your satisfaction?" he asked. "Three sugars and milk, correct?"

"No, it's good ... sir."

I took a sip from the cup—a very expensive-looking china cup. I was afraid I might drop it, so I was trying to be careful.

He poured three more cups—one for my mother, one for Jack and the third for himself—and passed them out.

"Before the hotel was taken over, they had a very fine afternoon tea every day. Special blends of tea, with crumpets and scones," Little Bill said.

"I've heard it was the most elegant tea this side of Buckingham Palace," my mother added.

"Yes, although they had some distance to go to actually meet the standards of the royal family," Little Bill said.

"I can only imagine what it would be like to have tea with the king and queen," my mother said.

"It is very pleasant," Little Bill said.

My mother gasped. "You've had tea with the king and queen?"

"Well, it wasn't just me," Little Bill said. "There were quite a few of us."

"Still, that would be … it would be … simply amazing."

"You would like to have tea at the palace?" Little Bill asked.

"Of course! Who wouldn't?"

I could think of at least one kid who might pass on that.

"Once this is over … this war … I shall arrange for a formal invitation to be sent to your family to have tea at Buckingham Palace."

My mother's mouth dropped open and she looked completely shocked, as though she couldn't believe her ears.

"You really don't have to do that … I wouldn't want to put you to any trouble."

"It would be no trouble at all."

"I don't know what I would even wear."

This wasn't the discussion I wanted to hear. I had a more pressing question. "Are we in trouble?"

Little Bill didn't answer right away, and with each passing second I got more and more worried. Maybe I could ask what *I* should wear to tea.

"No, you are not in trouble," he finally answered.

I let out a sigh of relief.

"In fact, I should offer my apologies for the rough manner in which you were brought here," he said.

"I still don't understand why they had to be tied up," my mother said.

Little Bill laughed. "My operatives might have argued that they should have been tied up *sooner*. If that had happened, perhaps there would have been one less broken nose. Not to mention the finger." He turned to me. "That bite went almost down to the bone."

"I'm sorry. We didn't know who they were!" I said. "When they took us, they—"

"No need to apologize. I had asked that you be brought to me, and they operated in accordance with normal procedures."

"But why didn't they just say they were bringing us to see you?" I asked.

"Would you have believed them?"

Jack and I exchanged a look.

"Probably not," Jack admitted.

"And then you might have run away or caused even more problems. We had to make sure it was done in a way that didn't alert or alarm your neighbours. That could have blown your cover and resulted in your family having to relocate again."

I hadn't even considered that we could be relocated again. That was an awful thought.

"I am, however, understandably concerned that it took seven or eight of my agents to subdue the two of you, and despite their numerical superiority, you still managed to inflict significant injuries on two of them," Little Bill said.

"That guy was lucky I only had *one* hand free," Jack said.

"That is nothing to brag about!" our mother warned him.

To be honest, I thought it was pretty good.

"I can't decide if it was an impressive show of your determination or of their lack of preparedness for the assignment. Or perhaps it was simply that they were lulled into a false sense of comfort, thinking they were only dealing with two young boys," Little Bill said. "Regardless, you must wonder about all of this. I imagine I'm the last person you expected to encounter."

"Close to the last," Jack admitted.

"Now, I must ask, how exactly did this all come to be?" he asked.

"Well, it wasn't exactly *our* idea," I said. "We'd be at home right now if these guys hadn't hauled us in. That was your idea, right?"

"Yes, I did ask them to bring you here, although I would have hoped for a more gentle transit. But I meant, more specifically, what transpired prior to you two being invited to attend here."

"If that was your idea of an invitation," Jack said, "I'd hate to see what happens when you really get rough with somebody."

Little Bill got a very serious look. "You *did* see what happens."

The image of that man being shot sent a chill up my spine. Of course we knew what could happen—this wasn't the first time we'd faced a life-and-death situation.

"Let me rephrase my question, then. How did you find yourself *needing* to be brought here? Please tell me, in detail, what transpired."

"We really weren't doing anything wrong," I said. "We were just waiting outside so our mother wouldn't have to walk home alone."

"You were waiting for me at this time of night? I would have had more than a few words for you when I saw you."

"Um … you wouldn't have seen us," Jack said.

She looked confused.

"We weren't going to meet you," I said. "We were going to sort of follow you … you know, stay out of sight but make sure you were okay."

"And why would you even think to do such a thing?" she demanded.

"It's late at night and Dad's always worried about you being out alone—"

"Your father told you to follow me?"

"Not exactly told us," Jack replied. "He said to keep an eye on you, and the only way we could do that was to watch out for you when you came home late."

She shook her head. "Did you really think that would work?"

"It has the other times that we've—" I stopped myself mid-sentence, but not before the damage had been done.

"You've done this *before*?"

I shrugged, and Jack shot me a dirty look. "A few times."

"But tonight you chose *not* to follow your mother," Little Bill said.

"That's right, sir," Jack said. "We saw that old man come out of the hotel, and he was carrying that bag, and then we saw somebody start to follow him."

"So you thought it would be wise for you to follow them."

"We thought that second guy might be up to no good," Jack said.

"Is that the only reason?" he asked.

"Well ... I guess we were sort of curious," I admitted.

"Thank you for being honest. So you initiated surveillance on the suspect."

"If that means following him, then yeah, that's what we did," Jack said. "We saw him turn down that alley and we followed him, and that's when things got all crazy."

"Yes, that was when things went in an unexpected direction," Little Bill said. "As you surmised, he was, in fact, up to no good. Our hope was to capture him ... alive."

"He's dead?" I asked, even though I really didn't have any doubts.

"Unfortunately. We did not expect him to pull a weapon and start firing. That was unexpected and unpredicted."

"Who was he, anyway?" Jack asked.

Little Bill didn't answer, and I realized that maybe he wouldn't tell us anything. He was probably unhappy about what we'd seen and that we knew as much as we now knew.

"You don't have to tell us," I said.

"Of course I don't have to tell you," he said. "But I will." He took a sip of his tea. "There are German sympathizers on this island. We were already certain of that. But we also believe that there are men and women who will do more than merely sympathize, who might be part of an established espionage ring. We set a trap tonight to test that theory. The theory proved correct, but unfortunately, with this man's death, we have no ability to extract further information."

Extracting information meant interrogating him and finding out things. Dead men were the only men who kept their secrets.

"And then, the second unpredicted and unexpected element emerged." He pointed at us.

"We didn't know what was going on," Jack said. "We saw that guy get shot, and then we tried to get out of there, and that's when the others spotted us. They were your men, right?"

"The same men who brought you here."

"If we'd known they were your men—you know, the good guys—we wouldn't have run away," I said.

"And we wouldn't have fought them, either," Jack added.

"You had no way of knowing," Little Bill replied. "I can understand your decision to flee when you saw a man being shot."

"That was pretty scary," I admitted. "But not as scary as when they shot at us."

"They shot at you!" my mother exclaimed.

Jack gave me another dirty look. When was I going to learn to keep my mouth shut?

"It was *way* over our heads," Jack said.

Sure, if a few inches counted as "way over."

"It was really more like a warning shot," Jack continued.

I knew neither of us believed that, but if it made her less worried, then a little lie was good.

"And how did you manage to escape?" Little Bill asked.

"We dodged into a walkway and then went into a building ... I think it was like a garage or storage shed," Jack said.

"Yes," Little Bill said. "That is what my operatives reported. But they did not know how you were able to elude them. Please explain that."

"That was Jack's doing," I said. "He threw open the door at the other end of the building to make them think we had run out that way, and we stayed in the building, hiding in the corner."

"Misdirection. Excellent. When they realized you hadn't gone in that direction, they doubled back and did a thorough search of that building."

"We weren't there. We doubled back, too, and went out through the door we entered," I said.

"Again, excellent thinking, Jack."

"That was George's idea," Jack said.

"It was an excellent idea. My congratulations."

"Thanks," I said. "But what I still can't understand is how they finally caught us, how they knew where to look, how they were at our house."

"Yeah, I was thinking about that," Jack said. "They didn't follow us—I know that—so how did they even *know* where we lived?"

"I told them," Little Bill said.

"But how did you know it was us to begin with?" I asked.

"When my operatives reported to me, they indicated that the shooting had been witnessed by two people who appeared to be young—perhaps even boys."

"But there are a lot of boys on the island," I said.

"Yeah, hundreds, maybe thousands," Jack added.

"But only two who could elude my operatives and vanish into thin air," Little Bill said. "And I happened to know the address of those two boys."

That explained everything.

"So, what happens now?" Jack asked.

"Now we wait," Little Bill said.

"Wait for what?"

"For your father to arrive."

"Our father?" I gasped. "Why is our father coming?"

"I thought it was necessary for him to hear about the changes that have become necessary because of what has happened." He got up. "It shouldn't be too much longer before he arrives."

Little Bill walked through the dining room and out the big double doors, leaving the three of us alone.

CHAPTER ELEVEN

WE SAT THERE in stunned silence. I was pretty sure we were all thinking the same thing—*what changes?*—but nobody wanted to say the words, like saying it would make it worse.

"I can't believe that Little Bill was here when all this happened," I said.

"He's here quite often," our mother said.

"He is?" I questioned.

She looked taken aback. "Maybe I shouldn't have said that. I hope I haven't violated any regulations."

"I don't think you saying he's here sometimes would be revealing any secrets," Jack said.

"Sometimes I'm not sure," she replied.

I knew that feeling. It had gotten to the point that I was trying to think everything through twice before I spoke. I wasn't that good at it, but it was becoming more of a habit, even with stupid things. The teacher would ask me if I'd had a good weekend and I'd wonder what I should and should not say, like me hanging around was a matter of national security.

"Little Bill comes through often," Mom said. "He always asks about you boys."

"That's nice."

"He really does think very highly of you two."

"It would have been nice if you'd told us he said hello," Jack said.

"He didn't say hello," Mom replied. "He just asked about you. I've even invited him to dinner but he said that would open the door to too many possible complications. Besides, sometimes I don't think he even eats."

"We know he drinks tea," I said, pointing at his empty cup.

"True, but he never seems to sit down long enough to eat, and the rumour is that he hardly ever sleeps," she said.

"Everybody sleeps," I said.

"Maybe, but it seems like he's always running from place to place, here, there, in Canada, in England. I'd have been surprised if he *wasn't* here when this happened," she said. She paused and then smiled. "Do you know what they call him around here?"

"Sir?" I asked.

She laughed. "God."

"God? Why would they call him God?" Jack asked.

"Because he sees all, knows all and seems to be everywhere at once …" She paused again and looked over her shoulder to make sure we were still alone. "Not that anybody would call him that to his face. Do you know that he remembers the name of every person who works here, asks details about their families, knows all about their backgrounds? I heard that he has a photographic memory."

"What's that?" I asked.

"It means his mind is like a camera. He looks at something and it sits in his mind like a photo in an album. He can flip to that page and see and remember everything, like he's looking at a picture," she said.

"Do you believe that?" Jack asked.

"If anyone's capable of that, it's him."

The big doors opened and our father entered, in uniform, followed by Little Bill. Dad rushed across the room. He looked worried. My mother got up and they hugged.

"Are you boys okay?" he asked.

"Yes, sir," Jack answered, and I nodded in agreement.

"Good." He turned to Little Bill. "Why did you have me brought here? Why are my children here?" He didn't sound happy.

"Please, have a seat," Little Bill said. His tone was friendly and he had a smile on his face. With most people, that would have only meant he *was* being friendly. But I remembered how Bill had told us that a good spy always acts really friendly and smiles before he kills somebody. Not that I thought he was going to kill my father, but it was still unnerving.

My father hesitated for a second and then sat down beside our mother.

"I know you must have many questions," Little Bill said.

"You've got that right."

"And I will answer them all, but first I must ask you to sign these forms." Little Bill slid some papers in front of my father.

He looked at them. "The Official Secrets Act? You want me to sign an oath of secrecy before you can tell me what's happening with my wife and children?"

"Yes, I must insist, or I'm afraid I can't even start this discussion."

"Who exactly are you?" my father demanded.

"Where are my manners?" Little Bill said. "My name is Stephenson, William Stephenson." He held out his hand and they shook.

"That's your name," my father said, "but you still haven't answered my question. Who are you? *What* are you?"

"I am, shall we say, in charge of operations at this hotel."

"You're the hotel manager?" my father asked.

Both Jack and I burst out laughing before we realized that wasn't wise or polite. We both shut up before our father had a chance to say anything.

"Forms, please," Little Bill said. He pulled a fancy pen out of his suit jacket and handed it to my father.

It looked as though my father was going to say something, or argue, or maybe even refuse. Instead he signed his name at the bottom.

"So?" my father asked.

"I am in charge—here on the island, throughout the Caribbean, in Canada and in Europe—of all activities that involve clandestine operations."

"Clandestine? That makes it sound like you're some kind of spy or something," my father replied.

"Yes," was all that Little Bill said in response. "And now, since you have signed the oath, it is time for you to know that I am not the only spy in the room."

My father looked around at the empty room—empty except for his own wife and kids—and then I saw his expression change as he realized exactly what Little Bill meant. "My wife is a spy?"

Little Bill nodded. "She is far more than a censor."

"But you never told me anything," our father said, looking at her.

"She couldn't tell you anything," Jack said. "You hadn't signed the oath."

"That is correct," Little Bill said. "And further, your boys could not tell you about what they have been involved in."

"What's next? Are you going to tell me my boys are spies, too?" he asked, and he started to laugh nervously.

"Yes, they have also been employed as spies."

My father stopped chuckling.

"Your sons are among the two most skilled, determined, bright and brave operatives I have ever been associated with."

"My boys?" Now he looked shocked, confused *and* concerned. I understood him feeling all of those things.

"I feel that keeping these secrets from you has been an unfair burden on your family. There should be no secrets between a husband and wife, no secrets between boys and their father," Little Bill said. "And that is why you were brought here today, why you were asked to sign an oath under the Official Secrets Act. You are going to be told everything."

I gasped.

"Isn't this what you wanted, George? To tell your father everything?" Little Bill asked.

"Yes, of course! I'm just not sure what we should say or where we should begin."

"You must tell him everything, and you should start at the beginning—with that first encounter at Camp X."

I covered my mouth as I tried to stifle another yawn. It was almost four in the morning and we'd been talking for more than three hours. With each passing hour and new story, my father's expressions and reactions had evolved. What had started as shock had changed to almost calm—although I think a big part of that calm was disbelief. And sometimes, when Jack was telling him something, I'd almost catch myself not believing it, either—even though I *knew* it was true because I'd been there.

We'd started off by telling him about how we had accidentally stumbled into Camp X, the super-secret spy base in Whitby ... how innocently it had begun, and then how our curiosity had gotten the better of us and eventually had almost gotten Jack and me killed when we got tangled up in a Nazi plot to infiltrate the camp. He'd asked a whole lot of questions all through that first story.

Then we'd gone on to explain that, to avoid Nazi retaliation against us, our family had been moved to Bowmanville and Mom had been assigned to work at the prisoner-of-war camp, Camp 30. We explained how we had become entangled in an escape plan, been kidnapped, been forced to crawl through a tunnel and nearly ended up on a U-boat headed for Germany.

The next story involved the gangsters who kidnapped Mom and threatened to kill her if we didn't help them break into Camp X to steal the gold deposits of the Bank of England that were supposedly stored there. By the time we got to that story, Dad wasn't asking nearly as many questions, but he did reach out and take Mom's hand, and he didn't let go of it again for the rest of the story.

Finally we got to how we'd broken up a plot to destroy the munitions factory at Ajax, and how that had led to us being sent to live in Bermuda.

By the end of the last story, Dad looked stunned. He just sat there, glassy-eyed, holding his face in his hands.

The door opened and Little Bill came in again. He had been doing that all night, every thirty minutes or so. He'd listen for a short while and then, without adding a word, leave. As the night went on, we all looked more and more tired and worn down. He didn't. Even now he looked refreshed, almost rested. Maybe Mom was right: he didn't need to sleep. Even his suit was neatly pressed, not a wrinkle, and his tie was perfectly knotted, the top button of his shirt still done up.

"I know this must be very hard for you to take in," Little Bill said to Dad.

He slowly shook his head. "You must admit, it all sounds pretty fanciful," he said. "My wife and boys are spies ..."

"Not really spies," he said. "More like operatives. And, technically, only your wife is an operative at this point."

"You mean her position as a censor?"

"I am afraid that is just her cover story," Little Bill said.

Now my father wasn't the only one who was confused and concerned. If Mom wasn't a censor ... what was she *really* doing?

"Your boys are quite amazing." Little Bill said. "They are remarkable young men, and what they have accomplished is truly astonishing. You should be very proud of them."

"I've *always* been proud of them."

I felt my chest sort of puff up. I looked at my father. He really looked as though he was proud of us.

"I have tried very hard to understand how they have been able to accomplish so much, and I have a number of possible explanations—theories, if you will. I believe that they are so adept not in *spite* of their age but *because* of their age," Little Bill said.

What exactly did that mean?

"Let me explain. Those who learn a second language in infancy are most skilled in that language. The younger you are when you acquire a it, the better you will speak it."

"But we only speak English," I said.

"I am not referring to your language skills," Little Bill said. "I am applying the same idea to the way that you are able, almost instinctively, to understand concepts of espionage."

"I get it," my father said. "Because they're young, it all comes more readily to them."

"Exactly," Little Bill said.

"I guess that makes sense," Jack agreed. "The younger you start, the better you should be at something."

"In theory," Little Bill said, "but there is also another factor. Not only do you two absorb concepts, but you are able to be calm in the face of danger." He turned to me. "Were you afraid last night, George?"

"Yeah," I said, before I thought to lie.

"Jack, were you afraid?" he asked.

"I guess so. You'd have to be *crazy* not to be afraid if a bunch of guys with guns are chasing you."

"Yet the fear did not cloud your judgment. You two were able to put aside fear, slow your heart rate, control your breathing and make the decisions that allowed you to escape. And for that ability you must thank your father."

We both looked at our dad. What did he have to do with last night?

"Captain Braun, have you told your family about your accomplishments in North Africa?" Little Bill asked.

My father didn't answer. His eyes fell to the ground.

"I thought not. You probably didn't want to worry them."

"There are some things that don't need to be known," my father said.

"I couldn't agree more," Little Bill said. "But tonight, we are going to disclose all, on the part of all members of the family. With your permission, I would like to tell your family of your deeds."

My father gave a weak little shrug in answer.

"While serving in North Africa, your father received almost a dozen citations for bravery and received three medals for his actions."

"Why didn't you tell us?" Jack asked.

"Or show us the medals?" I added.

"I was just being a good soldier," our father said.

"You were far more than simply a good soldier. You were a leader, a man who was able to stay calm under adverse conditions." Little Bill turned to my father. "Perhaps you could tell your family about what happened in Algeria."

"Lots of things happened in Algeria," he said.

"I was referring to the episode involving the three enemy tanks."

I sat up straighter and my ears perked up. This I wanted to hear.

"There's not much to tell. We destroyed some tanks and took some prisoners. We were doing what soldiers do."

"Modesty is a virtue, but false modesty is not necessary. I am afraid that maybe I need to tell the story ... with your permission."

My father nodded.

"Your father was in charge of a unit assigned to hold a position. Despite being tremendously outnumbered and outgunned and taking many casualties, your father was personally responsible for destroying three enemy tanks and for the subsequent capture of more than one hundred German soldiers."

Both Jack and I gasped.

"It's not like I was alone. I had good soldiers under my command ... the *best* soldiers under my command."

"Yet without your leadership, the entire position would have fallen, and you and your men would have been captured," Little Bill said. "You have a special ability to remain calm under enemy fire."

"Like us," Jack said.

Little Bill nodded in agreement. "And, of course, the very special skills that your mother possesses are also part of what you have inherited."

"What do you mean?" Jack asked. We both looked at our mother.

"I believe it would be better to show you, rather than tell you," Little Bill said. "And for that we need to wait until morning. I suggest that you all get some rest and we will continue tomorrow. Does that sound reasonable?" Little Bill asked.

"I'm certainly ready for bed," our mother said.

"Me too," Jack agreed.

"Maybe this will all make more sense after a few hours of sleep," my father added.

"Then we will reconvene at eleven o'clock," Little Bill said.

"Wait, I need to know something," I said. "You said that because of what happened, there were going to be changes. What sort of changes?"

"Those changes are being arranged right now. Until I have confirmation, I do not feel it would be proper to discuss it any further."

"When will you know?" I asked.

"Hopefully by tomorrow." Little Bill rose to his feet, signalling that it was time for us to leave.

CHAPTER TWELVE

THE HUSTLE AND BUSTLE of the dining room was becoming louder and louder. Around us, hundreds of people—almost all female—were having a cup of tea and a slice of toast before they started work. The mood was happy with lots of laughter, good-natured conversation and even singing. For the *ten-thousandth* time somebody came over to our table and my mother introduced them to our father and us. Apparently my father looked "very handsome" in his uniform, and Jack and I were either "cute, fine-looking young men" or "chips off the old block." Again and again we'd made polite conversation with some woman who knew my mother but was a stranger to us. There were also, in some cases, girls who weren't much older than Jack, just like in Ajax at the munitions factory. I sure hoped there was one big difference—I hoped that none of these girls were spies.

Now I started scanning the room, looking for suspicious behaviour. Maybe it was like Little Bill had said—this kind of thinking came naturally to me because we'd been exposed to it when we were so young. But it would have been restful to have been able to just sit here, sip my tea, eat toast with marmalade and *not* think about there being a spy behind every potted plant. I couldn't even remember what twelve-year-olds were supposed to think about.

We had spent the night at The Princess, Jack and I sharing a room. The biggest shock for me was that I slept so well. My head hit the pillow and I was gone until my mother gently shook me awake in the morning. Staying at the hotel had been convenient, but I couldn't help wondering if maybe there'd been more to it than that. It kept us in sort of a "safe house." What if the man who was shot had other agents working with him, and now we were in danger because someone had seen us that night? Was it possible that we'd been so focused on following him that we didn't notice that we were being followed, too? Had they tailed us back to the house and watched us being whisked away? I had too many questions swirling around in my brain. The only certainty was that with the guards and machine-gun nest and security at the hotel, this was a very safe place.

Yet those same guards that kept other people out also kept us in. Maybe Little Bill had arranged for us to stay here because he didn't want us going anywhere ... okay, now I was getting a little paranoid. I knew he'd always do the right thing for us. Of course, the right thing might mean that we would have to leave the island, maybe immediately, and that was why he hadn't let us go home last night. Were we going to be relocated again? Leaving the island wouldn't be the worst thing in the world—it wasn't like we'd been here very long. It would almost seem like it was a little vacation. The real question was where we'd be sent next. And more importantly, would our father be allowed to come with us, or would he be sent back to Africa? After all, he was a real hero, and they needed those over there to do the real fighting, didn't they? After having him back, and safe, was our unauthorized spying going to place him in harm's way, back into battle? I couldn't live with myself if that's what we'd caused. If this just ended well, I promised to try not to be curious ever again and ... there were too many possible options and no way I could figure things out ... I just had to stay calm and wait. What other choice did I have?

The dining room slowly emptied until there were no more than a dozen people scattered throughout the room, and the noise level died down. The only activity was the waitresses clearing away the dishes and wiping down the tables.

A woman entered the room through the main doors. She was older than anybody else we'd seen here, and her expression was stern and serious. She came straight toward us. I had a feeling we were about to meet another somebody-new who would think that I was "cute"—although judging from her expression, I doubted if she thought *anything* was cute.

"Good morning," she said. There was a formal quality to her voice and no hint of friendliness to her manner. "G is in his office. He'll see you in ten minutes."

"Thank you," my mother replied.

"Of course, you know the way," the woman said.

"Of course."

Without another word the woman abruptly turned and quickly walked away, as though she was late for a meeting.

"Who is G?" I asked.

"Little Bill," my mother replied.

"Why did she call him G?"

"G ... as in the first letter of God." She chuckled. "Not that you should ever call him that or refer to him that way within his earshot." She paused. "It's shorthand for his nickname. Not that it's meant in a bad way ... but I don't really know if he's aware of it."

I gave her a hard look. "Do you *really* think he doesn't know about it?"

"Well ... probably he does, but still. Finish up your toast and let's go. We don't want to keep him waiting."

I popped the last little corner of toast into my mouth and Jack tipped his cup and drained it.

"You have marmalade all over your face," my mother said to me. Before I could answer, she took a napkin, dipped the end in a glass of water and roughly wiped my face. Jack started to laugh—until she took the napkin and did the same to him, wiping both marmalade *and* the smirk from his face. I worked hard not to laugh—I didn't want that napkin aimed at me again.

We all got up, and my mother reached over and straightened my father's uniform tie. At least she hadn't used a napkin on him.

"Goodness gracious, can't I take the three of you anywhere without having to make sure you're presentable? We'd better hurry," she said. "I don't want to keep Little Bill waiting."

She took the lead and we obediently fell in behind. We went out the main doors of the dining room, but instead of heading right, toward the lobby, we turned left. We followed her down a long corridor that led to a set of stairs. At the bottom of two flights we came to a door guarded by two soldiers. They both saluted and my father returned the salute. Then one smartly opened the door.

We passed through, and we were in the basement ... long corridors leading off in two directions, lit by weak, yellowish bulbs.

"I was wondering," my father said. "Do you know his rank?"

"I'm not sure if he has a specific rank," my mother said. "Why do you ask?"

"I just need to know if I should be saluting him."

"I don't think that's necessary," my mother said, "but I do know I've seen him order around generals as if they were bellhops, and they instantly jumped to follow his commands."

"Maybe I'd better salute him, then, just to be sure," my father said.

"Maybe we'd *all* better salute him," Jack joked.

The corridor was warm and the air was very still, the overhead fans not producing much movement. We passed by an opening, and I was shocked to see dozens and dozens and dozens of women at long tables filled with hundreds, no, *thousands* of letters. In the few seconds it took to pass by, I could see that they were sorting the letters into little piles, like mail clerks.

We kept walking.

"It's pretty hot down here," Jack commented.

"I'm told it gets so hot in the summer that people faint," Mom said.

"I thought it was supposed to be cooler underground," I commented.

"But there's no air flow, and some of the spaces are pretty crowded."

There were other small rooms along the way—some no bigger than a little nook—and each was filled with people working away. Almost exclusively, they were women.

We turned a corner and there was the unfriendly woman, sitting at a desk. She looked up as we approached.

"Can I help you?" she asked.

"We ... we have an appointment," my mother said.

There was no look of recognition on her face—as if she hadn't just told us to come down. The woman looked at a book on her desk and ran her finger down the page.

"Please, go in," she said.

She reached under her desk and it looked as though she was pushing a button or something. The door popped open with a buzzing sound.

"Electrically controlled to restrict entry," she explained.

We went through the door. The room was tiny, not much more than a big broom closet, and Little Bill was seated at a desk, surrounded by filing cabinets. There were four chairs crowded in front of the desk. He was writing intently, so absorbed that he seemed not to notice our entrance.

"Captain Braun, reporting as ordered, sir!" our father said as he came to attention and gave a smart, sharp salute.

Little Bill looked up. "No need for that, Captain. Please be seated."

We jockeyed around each other and the chairs. Mom and Dad ended up in the middle, and Jack and I sat to either side. Little Bill continued to work for a few more seconds before he looked up.

"I trust you all had a good night's sleep," he said.

"Yes, our room was first class," my father said.

"Yes, lovely," my mother added.

"The Princess is ... was ... one of the most luxurious hotels in the world. I'm sure it will resurface as such after the war."

"Did you sleep well?" my mother asked him.

"Sleep?" He looked amused. "There will be time for sleep, hopefully, on the plane."

"You're leaving?" I asked.

"Shortly."

"Are you going back to Canada or ..." I let the sentence trail off because I knew he wouldn't be able to tell me.

"Time is short, so I must apologize for being very direct," he said. "In the past I have tried to keep things away from Jack and George. Yet despite the efforts of highly trained personnel and high security, they always seem to discover the very things we are trying to keep from them."

"It's more by accident than anything else," I said.

"Not by accident, but by design, temperament and ability."

"I don't understand," I said.

"It means that you are very good at finding out what I don't want you to find out. So we are now going to try another approach." He paused, and I felt as though our whole future hung on his next few words. "Rather than trying to keep you away from classified information, I am about to tell you everything."

"What?" Jack asked.

"I am going to tell you—all of you—everything that happens at the hotel."

"Everything?" I asked. That just didn't sound right.

"Perhaps not *everything*, because only God knows everything." He smiled. "And I mean the real God," he said, pointing toward the ceiling.

I burst out laughing.

"An interesting nickname they have affixed to me, although the person here most likely to know everything that happens is my secretary, the woman who let you into my office." He paused and lowered his voice. "Actually she's a little scary. I think if we really want to eliminate Hitler, we should put her in a plane, strap on a parachute and drop her behind enemy lines. She'd have things cleared up in a few days."

Now everybody was laughing.

"Come with me," Little Bill said.

He got up from his desk, and we stood as well. But then he turned and faced the wall behind his desk, and when he pushed against it, it slid open!

"I thought we'd take a little shortcut," he said, smiling at our shocked expressions. "This hotel is much more than it appears."

We followed him *into* the wall. A few bulbs hanging down from the ceiling dimly lit the space behind. He led us up a black metal spiral staircase. We spun around and around. When I looked up, it seemed to dead-end in cement blocks. I guessed then that another wall was about to open. Sure enough, when we reached the top of the staircase, Little Bill pushed against the wall that faced us and slid it over. Light flooded in, temporarily blinding me. We stepped out and into an office with comfy-looking furniture and big, bright windows at the top of the walls that allowed light in but didn't let anybody see in.

"Technically this would be my office," he said, "but I tend to spend more time down below. Much quieter. Do you know anything about the hotel?"

"Not really," Jack said.

"She's an impressive lady. Built in 1885, she is fondly referred to as The Pink Palace by Bermudians. She was built to provide an air of elegance, with the most exquisite furnishings. The Princess Hotel was, and I'm quoting, 'the height of modernity and comfort.'"

We left his office and were now in the lobby. "Queen Victoria's daughter, Princess Louise, visited the island in 1883. She told reporters that Bermuda was the Shangri-La of holiday destinations, and that put the island on the international travel map. She was a most gracious woman whom the islanders took to heart. This hotel, The Princess, is named after her, so it is known, more formally, as The Princess *Louise* Hotel."

I thought to mention that Louise was also the name of Jack's girlfriend, but decided it was better not to.

"Now, let us talk about the present. Tell me what you know about the wartime operations of the hotel."

"We don't know much," Jack said.

"Tell me the little you do know."

Jack shrugged. "Our mother works here, and letters travelling between North America and Europe or Africa are censored here. That's about it."

"Nothing else?"

"Um ... the letters are carried by planes ... sea-planes ... the Catalina flying boats, and they have to come here to refuel because no plane can cross the Atlantic in one jump."

"Correct. They must stop here, and then at the Azores for a second refuelling. And how do you know about that?"

"I guess from things my mother has told us, and what I hear from other people at school. We've even seen the mailbags being delivered from motor launches at the steps off the water."

"How did you see that?" Little Bill questioned.

"You can see a lot from the tops of the trees at the side of the hotel," Jack said.

"I wasn't aware of that. Perhaps those trees need to be trimmed. The letters are brought first to the basement. I believe you saw the sorting areas on your way to my office?"

"We saw them," I answered. That was where those women were sitting at the long tables.

"That is the first step. Letters are then directed to different areas in the building, depending on the priority and nature of the letter or package. Now, is there anything else that you know?"

Jack shook his head.

"George?" Little Bill asked.

"I know there's a lot more going on here than censoring letters," I said.

"And how would you know that?" he asked.

"The most obvious reason is that *you're* here," I replied, pointing at him. "You wouldn't be here if there wasn't more."

"That is one of the reasons I try not to make my presence too well known, which is why I couldn't visit you on my trips to the island. But do you have any other reason to suspect more?"

"What we saw last night. There wouldn't be spies, and guys following people, or guns, just because of some 'Dear John' letter.... Is this a spy school, like Camp X?"

"Judging from the difficulties our operatives experienced yesterday, it would be fair to assume that they do require additional training, but no, there is no spy school at this facility. The operatives assigned to this station are responsible for security throughout the island. Perhaps the best place to begin this discussion is to show you where your mother works."

We went up the main lobby staircase and along a corridor. There was thick carpet underfoot and lots of fancy pictures on the walls. I could see why a princess would like this place.

"Billy!" a man yelled. He rushed over and shook Little Bill's hand vigorously. He was little and so thin that it looked as though his clothes were hanging on him.

"It's good to see you, Ray," Little Bill said.

"And it's good to see all of you!" he exclaimed. He had an English accent and looked like somebody from a Dickens novel.

He shook my father's hand and then Jack's and then mine—taking it with both of his hands and practically shaking my arm out of the socket.

"I'd better get going now," he said. "I have places to go and people to—"

Little Bill reached out, grabbed Ray by the arm and spun him back around.

Little Bill held out his hand.

"Just having a little fun," Ray said.

He handed Little Bill a watch. It looked a lot like mine. I looked at my wrist. It was bare——my watch was gone!

Little Bill handed it to me. "Now the rest," he said.

Ray produced a second watch——it was my brother's—— and then a wallet. My brother didn't carry a wallet.

"That's mine!" my father exclaimed.

"If it's yours, how did it get into my pocket?" Ray asked.

"I ... I don't know," my father stuttered. He looked confused.

"You should try to keep it in your own pocket," Ray said. He handed it to my father.

"It was in my pocket!" my father snapped. "You're a pickpocket ... a thief!"

"I prefer to think of myself as a master craftsman," Ray said.

"It would be hard to argue with either position," Little Bill said. "Ray is in fact a thief, one who practises his craft in the service of king and country."

"To think, what's helping fight the Nazis is what got me in prison to begin with, and then got me out again."

"Yes, Ray was a guest of the government, serving a sentence that would still have close to ten years to run," Little Bill explained.

"But with time off for good behaviour, it could have been much shorter," Ray said.

"Or, in this case, using your bad behaviour in good ways," Little Bill said.

My father looked confused.

"So he steals for our side," I said. "Right?"

"Exactly, George," Little Bill replied.

"I still don't understand," my father said.

"I do," I said. "He can walk right up to practically anybody and take something from their pocket."

"He can. But he can also *put* that something back into their pocket," Little Bill said.

Now *I* was confused.

"He can not only steal something, but also replace it after it has been read and copied, so that the owner would never know the document had been out of his possession," Little Bill explained.

I could see where that would be an advantage. If they never knew it was gone, they wouldn't know that the information had been stolen.

"He is one of the best in the entire world," Little Bill said.

"One of the best?" Ray asked. He sounded offended. "By the way, Billy my boy, this is a bit embarrassing, especially for a man in my line of work, but I seem to have left my wallet at home this morning ... do you think you could lend me a pound or two?"

As soon as he said that, I figured I knew what he was *really* saying.

Little Bill reached into his jacket and searched, unsuccessfully, for *his* wallet. Ray had taken it without Little Bill knowing.

"*One* of the best?" Ray asked again.

Little Bill held out his hand for the wallet.

Ray held up his hands. "I don't have your wallet." He paused. "But I do have a suspicion," he said, his voice barely a whisper, "about where it might be." He looked at me. "I believe that young man may have stolen it."

"Me?" I exclaimed. "I would never take—"

"I think you should look in his jacket pocket ... front right."

I put my hand against my pocket. There was something there. I reached in and pulled out a wallet—a wallet that wasn't mine!

"I told you the boy was a thief!" Ray exclaimed.

"I didn't take it, honestly!"

"I know you didn't, George." Little Bill clapped his hands. "Bravo, Ray. I didn't feel that at all." He took the wallet from me and put it back inside his jacket pocket.

"So do you still think I am *one* of the best?"

"My apologies. Let me correct myself. Ray is the da Vinci of the craft of thievery. And that is just one of his many talents."

Now Ray was looking at me—hard, staring, as though he saw something wrong.

"What do you have there?" he asked.

"Where ... what?" I questioned anxiously.

He reached over and put a hand behind my head, and when he pulled it back, he was holding a watch.

Ray handed Little Bill the watch and he put it on his wrist.

"I don't think that boy has any *sense* whatsoever," Ray said, pointing at me.

Before I could even react, he reached behind my ear and produced a dollar bill—an American dollar bill!

"I told you he had no cents ... just a dollar. Here, this is for you," he said, handing me the dollar.

"Thanks."

"Don't thank me," Ray said. "You should thank him." He gestured to Little Bill. "I got the money from his wallet. That dollar as well as this money."

Suddenly a whole wad of cash seemed to appear magically in his hand.

"Here you go, Billy." He handed him the money.

Jack started laughing.

"Hey, hey, hey, I don't think you should be laughing," Ray said to Jack. "After all, you're not very bright."

He reached behind Jack's ear and a white dove was in his hand.

"See, the boy is nothing but a *bird*brain!"

Jack looked shocked, but everybody else laughed. Little Bill applauded.

"Ray is also a magician," Little Bill said. "And a safe-cracker and a locksmith and a master of disguise. He can change his appearance so you could walk right by and not notice him."

"Speaking of changing appearance," Ray said, "you two certainly are growing up. You look much older than you did only a few months ago."

"You've seen us before?" Jack asked.

"You're not the only ones who have spent time at Camp X."

"I'm sorry," Jack said. "I don't remember you."

"I don't even remember seeing you," I added.

"Oh, you saw me," he said. "I just looked a little different, that's all."

"Don't feel badly," Little Bill said. "I have walked past him more than once without recognizing him. All part of the job."

"Speaking of jobs, when will I be put to work again?" Ray asked.

"Tonight," Little Bill said. "A ship is being diverted to the harbour. There are some contents that need to be examined."

Ray rubbed his hands together in glee. "Can't wait. I'd better get my tools ready."

Ray reached out to shake Little Bill's hand again. Little Bill drew back his hand instead and the two men exchanged a smile.

"I'll see you boys around … although I doubt you'll see me."

Ray walked away chuckling and we continued on our way.

"We have a number of such men in our service."

"But can you trust them?" my father asked.

"Many have their faults, including the fact that they often have difficulty following directions, but their skills are far more beneficial than their faults are harmful."

We came toward a big double door. Directly in front stood two soldiers, rifles on their shoulders. They saluted sharply as we stopped. My father returned their salute, although I suspected it was Little Bill they were really saluting.

"Behind these doors is what we call Room 99. It is the most secure place in this entire facility, where the most important operatives are undertaking incredibly secret and important work. This is, of course, where your mother works."

CHAPTER THIRTEEN

THE GUARD OPENED THE DOOR and we walked in. It was a gigantic room and the entire space was filled with desks and tables and chairs, and it seemed each spot was occupied, in almost all cases by a woman. Everyone was working so intently that no one even looked up. We walked around the room and I looked down at the tables as we passed. There were letters on each desk and they were being closely examined. Some of the women were using gigantic magnifying glasses.

"The most significant letters and parcels found in the mail are brought to this room," Little Bill said.

"What makes one letter different from any of the others?" my father asked.

"Addresses are often the key. Certain addresses belong to known Nazi agents or sympathizers, and some general destinations are places of high enemy activity," Little Bill said.

"Like Spain?" I asked.

"Yes ... but how do you know that?" He looked at my mother.

"I would never tell him or anybody that," she said.

"I just know," I said. "It was in one of those newsreels that they show at the movies. There was something about Barcelona ... and some place in South America ... maybe Argentina."

"Yes, those are areas of high enemy activity. George, I don't know why I ever question what you know," Little Bill said. "Those letters or parcels with specific key indicators are secretly opened and searched for codes, secret writing, invisible writing or microdots."

"What's a microdot?" I asked.

"Let's see if I can show you." He looked around the room. "Can I have your attention, please?" Little Bill called out.

People stopped working and looked up.

"Is anybody presently assessing a microdot?" Little Bill asked.

A woman raised her hand. "I have one."

We walked over to her desk. She was holding a letter under one of those gigantic magnifying glasses. "Third line from the bottom, the punctuation at the end of the sentence," she said, passing her magnifying glass to Little Bill.

He leaned over the letter.

"Here, look here," he said.

Jack and I almost bumped heads trying to look. Jack backed away.

"What am I looking at?" I asked.

"The period at the end of the sentence."

I scanned the line until I reached the end of the sentence and looked at the period. It was a period. So what? Did he think it should have been a question mark or— There was something about it … it wasn't completely black … there were tiny, almost unnoticeable gaps, little white spaces and— "Is there a word printed on the period?" I asked.

"Not *a* word. *Many* words…. How many?" he asked the woman.

"Twenty or twenty-five," she said. "It's describing the—"

"You can put that in your report," Little Bill said, cutting her off.

He suddenly turned on his heel and walked away. We followed. He stopped at an empty desk—what might be the only empty desk in the room.

"This is your mother's workstation."

The top of the desk held nothing but a little basket, at the top right corner, with letters in it.

"I originally thought your mother could be a trapper," he said. "Those are the people, usually women, who are able to remove the contents and put them back, without the envelope showing any sign of tampering. And she was very good at that."

"But she doesn't do that now?" I said.

"We found she had an incredible talent for deciphering secret codes."

"Like Ireland?" I asked.

"What is Ireland?" my father questioned.

"It is a code where the first letter of each word forms a message. Very simple," he said. "But your wife has the ability to look at a letter, or the transcript of a radio message or what looks like a random series of numbers and letters and see patterns that most people can't see. I can't explain it."

"Neither can I," she said.

"It just seems to be a talent that some people possess," Little Bill said. "Often those people are math professors, or people who write or read mystery novels, or those who are very adept at crossword puzzles or playing Scrabble."

"She's unbeatable in Scrabble!" my father said. "I won't even play with her any more."

"My guess is that she should play with George instead," Little Bill said.

"Me?"

"Have you ever played Scrabble, George?" Little Bill asked.

"No, never."

He turned to my mother. "Try playing with George. I think he might put up a good game ... of course, I could be wrong."

I felt like asking when, but I kept quiet.

"Now, let me show you the rest of the operations based here at the hotel. They include monitoring and decoding radio signals, the counter-espionage team, those responsible for tracking U-boats, the forgers and ..." He stopped mid-sentence. "But first I think I should tell you what I am proposing for your family."

In the excitement of seeing and hearing everything, it had temporarily slipped my mind. That was the most important thing—what was going to happen to us?

"Perhaps we should go back to my office and—"

"No," I said, cutting him off. I needed to know the answer right away.

Little Bill looked surprised. My father looked shocked.

My mother spoke up. "George, where are your manners? You apologize immediately!"

I realized I'd crossed the line. I opened my mouth and—

"George is right," Little Bill said. "I should have started with that information ... it would have been more considerate of your situation. Let's just step out into the hall."

We exited through the big doors back into the hall. There was a grouping of wingback chairs in a small alcove overlooking the bay. Little Bill led us there and gestured that we should sit down. He stayed standing.

"You need to know that your mother's role is so *vital* that we cannot afford to allow her to be reassigned," Little Bill said.

That was good ... or was it? Just because my mother had to stay on the island didn't mean that my father did. Or us, for that matter.

I was almost afraid to ask, but ... "What about my father?"

"Yes, that is something we need to discuss." He looked at my father. "As of oh nine hundred hours this morning, you have been relieved of your duty at the dockyard and have been reassigned."

I felt like I'd been kicked in the gut. "Where ... where is he going?" I asked. Was he being sent off the island or back to Africa or to Europe or—?

"Starting tomorrow, your father will be second-in-command of the detachment stationed at The Princess Louise Hotel."

I laughed out loud!

"That way he will be able to keep an eye on his wife ... and everybody else here," Little Bill said. "I hope you approve of your new assignment."

"But what about the dockyards? That's an important position, a *vital* position," my father said.

"As is this. What transpires here is absolutely critical to the war effort, and we need to know that security will remain intact. This is an even more important position, and I can think of no better man to fulfill the role—someone who can keep a cool head in times of crisis. Do you accept the challenge?"

My father nodded his head and smiled slightly.

My mother reached out and took his hand, and they both smiled. Jack was smiling. I was smiling. This couldn't have worked out any better.

"Now, we have to discuss what will happen with your boys," Little Bill said.

I started. "Us? What about us?"

"I think we need to make some changes," Little Bill went on, "and I wish to discuss that with you two as their parents."

Jack got to his feet. "Nothing is going to happen to us without—"

"Without the permission of your parents," Little Bill said, cutting Jack off. "Sit down, please."

Jack hesitated for a split second as though he was going to argue, but he settled back into his chair.

"In the past it was necessary, unfortunately, for your boys to be involved in things without your permission and without your knowledge. Now, however, we not only can, but *should*, have parental permission."

"What are you suggesting?" my father asked.

"I would like to employ the boys here at the hotel," Little Bill said.

"You want *us* to work here?" I gasped.

"They can't work here. They have to go to school!" my mother exclaimed.

"Yes, I have to agree with my wife," my father said.

"I am proposing that they do both. They would work here an occasional evening and sometimes on the weekend," Little Bill said.

"We could do that," Jack said.

"Yeah, we could," I agreed.

"And we would insist that they maintain high standards at school," Little Bill said. "Should we insist on a B average as a minimum?"

"But that's better than I usually get!" Jack objected.

"Then maybe it is time to *raise* your average," Little Bill suggested.

"I agree," my mother said. "A B average is the acceptable minimum."

"Do you think you can do that?" my father asked Jack.

Jack let out a sigh. "If I have to, I can."

"If he can't and I can, can I still work here?" I asked.

My parents laughed, and Jack shot me a look that could kill.

"We'll cross that bridge if we come to it," Little Bill said. "There are also other conditions. We would expect you both to continue with activities expected of young people, to allay suspicion. You will remain on the rugby team ... by the way, excellent game last week, Jack."

"Thanks," Jack replied. "But how did ...?"

He let the sentence trail off. Of course, *God* knew everything.

"And, George, for being among the youngest players on the pitch, you show great spirit and bravery."

I nodded. What could happen to me in a rugby game that could compare to what had happened to me in real life? Nobody on the rugby pitch carried a gun.

"Have you seen us play?" Jack asked.

Little Bill smiled. "A few minutes, perhaps a quarter of a game. It is also important that you continue to have friends of your own age. Louise, for example."

"Who is Louise?" my father asked.

Jack blushed. "She's a girl."

"I didn't think she was a bird," my father said.

"Perhaps your *girlfriend* could come to the house for dinner one night?" my mother suggested.

Jack looked incredibly embarrassed and stared at the floor.

"Are the conditions we've outlined acceptable? Would it be all right for your boys to spend time working at the hotel?" Little Bill asked then.

Jack and I looked at our parents, and they looked at each other. I wanted to will them into saying yes, because they didn't look completely convinced.

"I assure you that all of their activities will be *within* the hotel. There will be no assignments outside of the facility," Little Bill added.

"Well ..." my father said.

"And with the security we have here, including yourself as second-in-command, there is virtually no safer place on the island."

"That's a point," my father agreed.

"But what will they be doing?" my mother asked.

Good question. Would we be reading letters, checking for secret codes, looking for enemy agents?

"Mainly they'll be moving mailbags, sweeping, emptying the garbage cans and—"

"You want us to empty garbage cans?" Jack asked.

Little Bill furrowed his brow. "What did you think you would be doing?"

"I don't know ... stuff. You said we had special skills."

I nodded enthusiastically in agreement.

"There is no argument about that. The only question is this: should we be employing young people to exercise those skills?" Little Bill said.

"I don't think so, if my opinion counts for anything," my father said.

"It counts for *everything*," Little Bill said. "That and the opinion of your wife."

"I agree with my husband."

"But, Mom, we should—"

Jack was silenced by a look from our father.

"Then that is what you will be doing here. You must remember that all people employed here, regardless of their job, are helping the war effort. But if you don't want to—"

"We'll do whatever you want us to do!" I exclaimed, cutting him off. "That is, if we're allowed to."

"I think that would be all right," my father said.

"But those marks had better stay high," our mother warned.

"They will!" Jack said. "I promise."

Our mother smiled. "When do you want them to start?"

CHAPTER FOURTEEN

"COULD YOU PLEASE pass the vegetables?" Louise said.

"Certainly," my mother said as she flashed a big smile at her.

My mother loved manners, and Louise had enough good manners for four people. Actually her manners made me kind of nervous. I was afraid to burp, and I'd tried really, really hard not to slurp my soup.

"It is so nice to be part of a family meal," Louise said. "Not that Mrs. Farrow isn't a wonderful person—she's very nice—it's just different being with a family."

"It's very nice for us to be together," my mother said. She reached out and squeezed both my hand and Jack's.

Jack turned a little red and squirmed slightly in his seat. I figured Mom wasn't the person he wanted holding his hand.

"I know it's hard to be away from home," our father said. "I must be the luckiest man in the whole army to be able to go home each night to have dinner with my family."

"We're pretty lucky ourselves," our mother said. She released our hands—Jack quickly drew his away and under the table as Mom gave Dad a big, warm smile.

"It's unfortunate that you couldn't stay with your parents," my mother said.

"I *wanted* to stay," Louise said, "but they said it was too dangerous."

"The bombing is devastating London," our father said. "Hundreds are being killed and—" He stopped as he realized what he was saying. "I'm sure your parents are fine."

She nodded politely, a sad, faint smile on her face.

"I know that if my family were in London, I'd want them to get away from the bombing. I'd want them to be someplace safe ... like here," my father said.

"That's what my father said, too. He just wanted me to be safe."

"Sometimes parents make decisions based on what they know is best for their children, even if those decisions involve sacrifice," our mother said. "I'm sure it's hard on your parents, as well."

"I know it is," Louise said. "My mother sends me letters and she tries to be brave, but I can read between the lines."

I stifled a chuckle and Jack shot me a dirty look. I wasn't chuckling about her or what she'd said, it was just that I was *sure* she couldn't read between the lines as well as our mother could.

"It would have been good if your parents could have come with you," Jack said.

"They couldn't," Louise said. "My parents have to be in London … for work."

"What do your parents do for a living?" our father asked.

"They … they work for the … for the government," she replied. She looked nervous and her eyes fell to her plate. Why would that make her so nervous? And why did her being nervous make me nervous … no, not nervous … suspicious.

"Both of them? Well, I guess we all work for the government these days," our mother said.

"Yes, I guess so," she mumbled. She looked very uncomfortable. But why? She was acting like she was lying, but there was no reason to lie about what your parents did for a living … unless …

"What do they do for the government?" I asked.

"I'm not really sure, actually."

"You don't know *what* your parents do?"

"Well … not exactly … specifically."

"How about in general? What line of work are they—?"

"My son is naturally inquisitive," Mom said, cutting me off with a sharp glare.

"I have a few other words to describe him," Jack said.

"Enough," my father said sharply. "There's no reason why *both* our sons have to be rude. George, you need to apologize right now."

"It's all right," Louise said. "Honestly! George was just interested, making conversation. I'll ask them in my next letter and let you know once they reply."

"That's really not necessary," my mother said.

"It is!" she exclaimed. "Now that George has brought it to my attention, I think I really ought to know, don't you? Thank you so much, George."

"Um … you're welcome."

"And when you do write your mother, please let her know that she has done an excellent job of raising a fine young woman," my mother said.

"That is so kind of you," Louise said. She smiled broadly—which was very nice, but could also be very deceptive. A bright smile could hide a lot.

"Do you have any other questions, George?" she asked. "I'd be happy to answer them."

The only questions I wanted to ask, I couldn't—not that she would give me honest answers if she were, as I was beginning to suspect, some sort of spy.

"No, I'm good," I said.

"In that case," my mother said, "you and Jack can clear the table."

I quickly got up. Any excuse to leave was a good one. I piled up some of the dishes, scraping the scraps of food onto the top plate. Jack was gathering up the serving bowls. Slowly, carefully, I walked out of the dining room and pushed through the door to the kitchen. I put the dishes in the sink. I had to bring them in, but I didn't expect I'd have to wash them.

I heard the door open and Jack came in. He put the serving bowls on the counter as I scraped the food from the plates into the garbage and—

"Owwww!" I yelled as he punched me in the arm.

"What were you doing—?"

"What's happening in there?" my father called through the closed door.

Jack and I exchanged a look. "I just ... dropped a fork on my toe."

There was no answer from the other room. Either they believed me or they didn't want to call me on a lie.

"Quit being a jerk," Jack muttered.

"Hey, *you* punched *me*!"

"Believe me, you leave her alone or that was just a little taste of what you'll get," he threatened.

"Go ahead, try it," I said. "I can yell louder than that, and Dad is on the other side of that door."

"He won't always be on the other side of that door. Are you planning on walking to school with me tomorrow?"

"Not if I can help it." Not that I had much choice. Maybe it would be better to try to explain before he got any angrier.

"Look, I was just asking questions because——"

"She is *not* a spy," he said, cutting me off. "Stop thinking that everybody is a spy!"

"I don't think everybody is a spy," I said. "Mainly just girls who date you."

His eyes flashed with anger. Maybe I could leave early tomorrow and walk to school by myself.

"Didn't you notice how she was acting?" I asked. "She seemed nervous and she wouldn't answer my question."

"Maybe she couldn't answer your question," Jack snapped.

"What does that mean?"

"If somebody asked you what Mom did, what would you say?" Jack asked.

"I'd say she works at the hotel."

"And if they asked what she *specifically* does, would you tell them?"

"Of course not."

"Maybe Louise can't say anything, either," Jack said.

"Are you saying her parents are like spies or something?"

"Maybe."

"Now who's the person thinking everybody is a spy?"

"I'm not saying they're spies, but we know that not just anybody sends their children to a fancy place like Bermuda, so who knows what they do?"

He did have a point. Not that I was going to admit it.

"So just shut up and stop asking her questions. Okay?"

"I guess so."

"Besides, you shouldn't be asking questions like that in front of Mom and Dad," Jack said. "That is, if you want to keep working at the hotel."

"What's that got to do with anything?"

"Think about it. They were nervous about us getting into any more spy stuff and we agreed that we'd just be regular kids—or at least pretend to be—and now you're practically conducting an interrogation out there."

I hadn't thought of that. Another good point.

"Well?" Jack asked.

"I won't ask her any more questions," I promised.

"Good."

Jack turned and went back into the dining room. I wouldn't ask any more questions—at least out loud— but I'd still keep my eyes open. After all, like Little Bill said, it was in my nature!

CHAPTER FIFTEEN

I PUSHED THE CART along the hall. The carpeting cushioned the wheels and I moved silently. I liked to practise moving without making any noise. I left the cart at the open door and went into the room. There were three women at a desk, magnifying glasses in hand. They barely noticed me. I picked up the almost-full garbage can, brought it back to my cart and dumped its contents into the big bin. I tapped the bottom of the can to make sure the last bit of garbage fell out. Another mission accomplished. Another garbage can emptied for democracy, another blow against the Nazis, another ... who was I fooling?

I brought the garbage can back in and placed it on the floor. One of the women *almost* looked up. I went back to my cart and pushed it to the next door. I tried to open it but it was locked. That was strange. It was usually unlocked, sometimes even open. I knocked on the door, gently at first and then a bit louder, but there was no answer.

"You want in there?"

I turned around, startled. It was Ray. He had come up so quietly that I hadn't heard him. Apparently I wasn't the only one who could move silently.

Since I'd started working here three weeks ago, I'd run into Ray a dozen times. He was always friendly and really, really interesting. If he wasn't pulling a dove out of his pocket, he had card tricks he wanted to show, or he was dressed like a sailor or a waiter. I liked him. I didn't think my mother liked him much, because he was "a criminal." She hadn't actually said anything, but I could tell.

"You trying to get in there?" Ray asked again.

"I have to collect the garbage."

"So do you want to get in?"

"It's locked."

Ray got a confused look. "That's not what I was asking. Let me ask it again. Do ... *you* ... want ... *in* ... there?"

"It ... is ... *locked*," I replied, using that same exaggerated pace and tone of voice. I rattled the doorknob to emphasize the point.

"Why don't you just use a key?" Ray asked.

"I don't have a key." Did he think I was stupid?

"Sure you do. It's right in here."

Ray reached around me into the big garbage bin and rummaged around in the papers. Did he really think I had a key and had thrown it away? Maybe he really did think I was stupid.

"Here it is," he said. He held aloft a paper clip.

"That's a paper clip."

"That's where you're wrong, me boy. It *is* a key." He took the paper clip, straightened it and then twisted it differently. "Doesn't it look like a key now?" he asked.

"It looks *less* like a paper clip," I admitted, "but not more like a key."

"Here, take it."

I held out my hand and he dropped a candy in it. Where was the paper clip?

"No, that's not it. Here, take this," he said.

This time he put a coin in my hand. Then a pen, and a handkerchief and an egg ... where did he get the egg from?

Ray chuckled. "Okay, seriously, just watch."

He held up the paper clip, waving it in the air like a conductor leading an orchestra. Then he dropped to one knee in front of the door. He inserted the paper clip into the keyhole and wiggled it around. There was a loud click, and he pushed open the door!

"How did you do that?" I exclaimed.

He held up the paper clip again. "Remember, I had a key. You can get the garbage now."

"Okay, thanks." I went to open the door and bumped into it. It was locked again.

"It's locked," I said.

"I know. I locked it again, but you can get in. Here."

He went to hand me the paper clip but I drew back my hand.

"I can't open a door with that."

"You don't know until you try. Here ... I'll show you."

He pulled me down on my knees beside him, in front of the door.

"If you think about it, a key is just a piece of metal that turns the little tumblers in the lock, moving them from one position to another. That's what this is. Here."

He handed me the paper clip again and this time I took it.

"Now the first part ... the important part," he said, "is that you have to place it in the keyhole."

"Oh, yeah, of course." I did that.

"Now you have to feel the clip against the metal of the lock and listen for the sound. Put your ear close to the lock."

I bent nearer.

"And close your eyes," he said. "It will help you hear better."

That didn't make any sense but I did what I was told. I still didn't hear anything ... well, maybe something.

I could hear the tiny tap, tap of the clip against the metal. Ray put his hand on top of mine.

"Just jiggle it a little and—"

This time there was a loud click. Ray turned the knob and the door opened.

"Not bad," he said.

"It wasn't like I did anything."

"You were almost there. Just keep practising." He handed me the paper clip and walked away, humming to himself noisily.

I stood up and went to drop the paper clip into the big garbage bin and then stopped myself. I looked at the clip and put it in my pocket instead.

CHAPTER SIXTEEN

"WHAT ARE YOU DOING?" Jack demanded.

I jumped to my feet in surprise. I'd been kneeling at the front door of our house, so intent on trying to pick the lock that I hadn't heard him coming.

"Were you searching for a lost penny, or saying a prayer?"

"You know exactly what I was doing," I said.

"If you think you can pick that lock, you really should be saying your prayers, because the only way you're getting that door to open is with divine intervention."

"What does that mean?" I questioned.

"God is going to have to open the door for you, like he parted the Red Sea for Moses, because you're not going to do it by yourself."

"O ye of little faith."

"Faith I have. Brains I also have. And you're not going to open it."

"I might be able to do it," I said. I'd only been working at it for about fifteen minutes. That wasn't *that* long.

"Then you just keep trying, but I'm going through the back, which I know isn't locked. If you like, I'll even show you how to turn the knob and open the back door, which is, like I said, *unlocked*."

"Any fool can go through a door that's not locked," I said.

"Sounds to me like the real fool is the person trying to pick a door that's locked instead of going in through the one that's unlocked."

"I'm practising."

"Give it up. You're not Ray," Jack snapped.

"I never thought I was, but at least I'm trying to learn instead of wasting my time with some dizzy dame."

"Time spent with Louise is never a waste," he said. "Spending time with you would fall into that category, and I'm not going to waste any more." He started to walk away and then stopped. "What are you using to pick the lock?"

I showed him my "pick." Ray had given it to me. It was a thin piece of metal, sort of like a very thin pencil—actually it was painted to look like a pencil. Ray had told me that it was illegal to carry "burglary tools" so it was best to make them look like something else.

"If you jam the lock with that, Dad isn't going to be happy."

"Neither will I," I admitted. "Weren't you leaving?"

"Gladly. I'll be the guy *inside* the house, sitting in Dad's comfy chair and sipping lemonade. Of course since that is a door and not a window, you won't be able to see me."

Jack walked away, chuckling to himself. It was good that he at least found himself funny.

I went back to work. Before he'd come up, I was ready to quit. Now I couldn't. I knew that if I had enough time, I could pick this lock. That wasn't just wishful thinking. Ray had given me a couple more lessons and helped me practise. Since then I'd picked the lock on three different rooms at the hotel, the neighbour's back door—thank goodness they weren't home and hadn't seen me—and even the side door of our school. I was getting faster and better.

I wiggled the pick around in the lock. This one was stubborn. But then the lock clicked loudly! I almost screamed, I was so excited. I reached up and turned the knob, and the door opened!

I jumped to my feet and stepped into the house. I didn't see Jack, but I could hear him moving around in the kitchen. I went to close the door, but thought better of it. I left it open and went over and sat down in the chair Jack was planning to occupy.

Jack walked in, whistling to himself, holding a glass of lemonade. He saw the open door before he saw me. He stopped dead in his tracks, the whistling replaced by a shocked expression.

"Since you're up anyway, could you close that door?" I asked innocently.

He looked like he was going to argue, and then it passed. He went over and closed the door.

"You did it," he said, like he couldn't believe what he was seeing.

"I told you I could pick that lock. It's not that hard. Ray's a good teacher."

"Do you think he could teach me?" Jack asked.

"He could if you were around more." Lately Jack had been spending more and more time with Louise, while I worked at the hotel. And often Ray was around, so I spent time with him.

Ray seemed to always be interested in what was going on, so excited about things, like a little kid with a new toy. And he had lots of new toys that he showed me. He had a pair of sunglasses with little mirrors so you could see behind you without turning around. He showed me a book and a newspaper that had special holes—too small to be detected but big enough to see through when held in front of your face. He had a pack of cigarettes that was actually a camera, and a trench coat with secret pockets and a fedora that held twenty feet of thin, strong cord for getting up to or down from a second- or third-storey window.

"Maybe this weekend Ray could teach you," I suggested.

"Maybe if he's there on Saturday. I can't go in on Sunday. I'm having dinner at Louise's house. Mrs. Farrow invited me."

"Forget lock picking, then. You'd better brush up on your manners."

"I've got manners," Jack said. "Besides, it's not like I'm meeting her real parents."

"Have you found out what her real parents do for a living?"

He didn't answer. Maybe she hadn't told him, or—

"I know," he said quietly.

"What? What do they do?" I asked.

"Just because I know doesn't mean that I'm going to tell you. A promise is a promise, and I promised Louise I wouldn't tell anybody," he replied.

"I'm not anybody, I'm your *brother*."

"Which means you're a *no*body. I keep my word." He paused. He had a smug little smile on his face. "But I can tell you that you'd be pretty impressed if you knew."

"Like I care."

"You would care. But I'm not telling."

"I wouldn't care if she was the daughter of the king and queen of England," I said defiantly.

Jack snorted. "Oh, you'd care, believe me ... but I can't tell you anything. It's on a need-to-know basis, and you don't need to know anything."

"Maybe I don't want to know anything."

"Oh, you do," Jack said. "I can see it in your eyes."

"Yeah, right."

"I could tell you," Jack said, "but then I'd have to kill you." He laughed at his lame little joke.

"Maybe there are some things happening at the hotel that I'm not telling *you* about," I replied.

"Yeah, like you're dumping some top secret garbage or sweeping some Nazi dust from the floors?" Jack asked.

"I do more than that."

"Sure you do. But anyway, I'd rather spend time with Louise on the beach than with Ray at the hotel."

"Ray is a lot more interesting than Louise," I said.

He put a hand on my shoulder. "You really are still a kid, aren't you?"

Maybe he was right. But if I'd learned one thing from Jack, it was that girls could be trouble, and I had no difficulty finding trouble on my own.

I brushed his hand away. "I may be young but I'm not stupid. You don't have to come to the hotel any more at all. Your loss. Just more time for Ray to show me more neat stuff and teach me more tricks of the trade."

"What's he showing you?" Jack questioned.

"Sorry ... need-to-know basis ... wouldn't want to have to kill you."

"Who cares? It's not in my plans to become either a magician or a safecracker. Which one are *you* hoping to become?"

"Maybe both. I have to decide which one has the most money in it."

"Just don't tell Mom and Dad. I don't think they like Ray very much."

There was nothing to think about there—Mom had been pretty clear she didn't like me hanging around with him. That wasn't going to stop me, though. I'd just have to make sure she never found out.

CHAPTER SEVENTEEN

"YOU HAVING FUN?" Ray asked.

I looked up from the garbage can I was getting ready to empty.

"Yeah, lots of fun."

"I just think it's such a waste of talent to have you emptying the rubbish."

"I'm glad somebody besides me thinks that," I agreed. "There are hundreds of things I could be doing instead."

"I agree," he said. "Instead of you handling the rubbish bins, they could have you making beds or sweeping floors or—"

"Very funny."

"I try," he said and gracefully bowed. "Perhaps rather than a magician, I should be a comedian ... maybe I could entertain the troops."

"Speaking of troops ... when did you become a soldier?" I asked.

Ray was in uniform. I looked at the emblems on his sleeve—he was a general!

"It was a sudden decision to enlist, and imagine that, my first day and I'm already a general. Maybe tomorrow I might be supreme commander of all the Allied forces! If you see any more little stars being thrown in the garbage, you grab them for me and I'll have a battlefield promotion."

"Where did you get that uniform from?" I asked.

"Downstairs, the tailor shop. They can make practically any costume I want."

"I don't think most soldiers would like you calling it a costume. I'm surprised nobody objects to you wearing a uniform."

"Why should they?" he asked, looking genuinely surprised. "The Pope doesn't object when I dress like a priest."

"You've dressed up as a priest?"

"Heck, I've dressed as a nun."

"You're joking ... aren't you?"

He shook his head and a crooked little smile appeared.

"Now, back to my original question. Are you having fun?" he asked.

"Does it look like this is fun?"

"Don't imagine it is, so put down the rubbish bin and come with me."

I put it down. "What are we going to do?"

"Weren't you listening? We're going to have some fun. Do you think your brother wants to come have some fun, too?"

Part of me wanted to say no because he was being such a pain, but maybe joining us would get him more interested in coming to the hotel.

"He would like that," I said. "I think he's in the ballroom, washing the floors."

"Now that really is fun, but we'll try to tempt him away. Let's go."

I happily—but warily—trailed after Ray.

We went through the service corridor and then into the kitchen. It was—as always—busy. There were lots of people preparing food and drink for the staff. We passed through unnoticed and went out into the ballroom. The tables had been pushed to one side and the chairs stacked up so Jack could wash the floor. It looked as though he was almost finished.

Jack turned at the sound of us entering. He gave a little wave in our direction.

"Jack, me boy, put down that mop and come with us," Ray called out.

Jack didn't seem to need further encouragement. He let go of the mop and it dropped to the floor with a crash.

Ray led us out the back door of the kitchen, past the big trash bins—I was very familiar with them—and into the gardens that lined the seawall. We caught up with him at the stairs leading to the bay—to the place where the mail-bags were brought for sorting, censoring and searching in the hotel.

That was it? He wanted us to carry bags up to the hotel? Well, it certainly wasn't very exciting, but probably better than being on garbage duty.

We stopped at the top of the steps. There was a small motor launch, with two sailors in it, but no bags.

"Do you boys want to know what I have in mind?" Ray asked.

"I want to know," Jack said, "but whatever it is, it has to be better than mopping."

"It is," Ray said reassuringly. "In fact, rather than mopping the ballroom, you're going to be sweeping that ship." He gestured to a vessel anchored in the bay.

"That doesn't sound much better," Jack said.

"Actually it's much better. That ship was forced into port by a corvette. It sailed from Barcelona and was en route to South America. Do you know why it was forced into port here?"

"There could be lots of reasons," Jack said.

"There could be, but in this case it has to do with treasure. We have reports that the ship is carrying treasure."

"Like diamonds and gold?" I gasped.

"Much more valuable."

"What's more valuable than that?"

"Art. We received reports that the ship is carrying paintings the Nazis have taken from museums and are sending to South America to be sold."

"Why would they do that?" Jack asked.

"For the same reason anybody sells anything: money. They sell the art and use the money to purchase materials needed for their war effort. Our job is to sweep the ship and look for where they've hidden the treasure," Ray explained.

"So you didn't mean we were going to sweep it with a broom," I said.

"Not quite," Ray said. "Are you two in?"

"Of course we're—"

"Shouldn't we get permission first?" I asked, cutting Jack off.

"You have permission," Ray said. "From me."

"I was thinking that maybe ... maybe we should ..."

"Check with our mommy?" Jack said, a smirk firmly planted on his face.

"We're really not supposed to leave the grounds of the hotel," I said.

"You're hardly leaving the grounds," Ray argued. "It's right there."

"I still think we should ask Mom."

"You *could* do that," Ray said. "Of course, if you did, what do you think she'd say?"

Jack and I both laughed. There was no question about her answer.

"I don't think she'd be too happy," I said.

"And it's not real smart to make her unhappy," Jack added.

"Then we have a perfect solution," Ray said. "Don't tell her. We won't be gone long. She won't even notice."

Jack and I exchanged a doubtful look.

"And if you think about it, you have permission," Ray said. "*My* permission. And I'm a general, which definitely outranks a mother."

"Not our mother," I said. "Besides, you're a fake general."

"Well then that fits perfectly, because I'm only giving you fake permission." He laughed. "Come on. You'll be perfectly safe. The passengers and crew of the ship have been escorted ashore, so the only people on board are our agents. Don't worry, you won't get caught."

"My parents have eyes in the backs of their heads," I said.

"That won't be a problem. Your father is off the grounds up in Hamilton at a meeting, and your mother is locked inside Room 99 working on a mystery."

"How do you know that?" I asked.

He smiled. "I know lots of things. I also know you'll be back ashore, mopping and collecting garbage, before either of them notices. Besides, you can think of this as part of your ongoing education. I'm going to show you boys how to crack a safe."

"I'm in," Jack said. He started down the first few steps, stopped and turned around. "You coming?" he asked me.

I didn't see that I had much choice—thank goodness.

CHAPTER EIGHTEEN

I SLOUCHED DOWN in the seat of the motor launch as it moved away from the pier. I wanted to make sure that my mother didn't see us. Pretty soon we were far enough away that she wouldn't be able to tell it was us. The sound of the motor subsided to a rumbling, bubbling sound as we neared the ship.

It was big ... not gigantic, but big ... and it was mainly white with splotches of rust. Its name—*Conquistador*—was painted on the side in rusting letters. Up close you could tell that the ship was old, and pretty beat up. We pulled in beside a rope ladder hanging from the ship, and one sailor grabbed onto it and secured the motor launch while the second one killed the engine.

"You first," Ray directed.

I tried to stand up but almost tumbled overboard as the boat rocked to the side. Jack grabbed me and stopped me from falling.

"Slick move," he said under his breath.

I grabbed the ladder and started up. It had rope sides and wooden steps, and it swayed as I climbed. I didn't like heights, and it was a *long* way up. I got to the top and there was a soldier, a rifle on his back, standing guard. He offered me a hand and pulled me up and onto my feet.

"Must be desperate for help if they're sending kids," he said.

"How old are you?" I asked.

"Twenty ... on my next birthday," he said.

"Yeah, so look who's talking," I snorted.

Before the soldier could respond, Jack appeared at the top of the ladder and he offered him a hand. When Ray appeared, the soldier snapped to attention and saluted.

"How about less saluting and more helping," Ray suggested. The soldier jumped forward and helped Ray aboard.

"We need to go to the special quarters," Ray said.

"This way, *sir*," the soldier replied. "I'll show you, sir."

He led and we followed.

I fell in beside Ray. "Doesn't he recognize you?" I whispered. "Doesn't he know you're not a real general?"

Ray shook his head. "Most people only look at the stars on the sleeve, not the face above them," he said quietly, so the soldier couldn't hear him. "It's the same with priests. They only look at the collar."

"How big is this ship?" I asked.

Ray tapped his stars. "Sorry, can't help you. I'm in the army, not the navy. If I had decided to wear an admiral's uniform, I could have told you everything."

"No, seriously."

"Seriously. I have no idea. I just know it's not my job to search the whole ship. I'm only responsible for the safe in one of the cabins."

"And the rest of these guys, they have to search the whole ship?" Jack asked.

"Every square inch."

"How long have they got?" I asked.

"Twelve hours, and then they have to let the ship go on."

"Can they really search the whole thing in that time?" Jack asked.

"They have a lot of people going over it with a fine-tooth comb," Ray said, "but again, I'm only interested in the safe."

As we walked, following the soldier, the ship rocked slightly with the waves, and I kept a hand on the wall of the corridor. As we passed each open door, I saw people inside, moving, sorting, searching.

What I also noticed was the condition of the ship. The walls were pocked and rusted and desperately needed to be scoured and painted. There was dirt and grime on the floor, and I suddenly feared that they *had* brought me here to sweep and clean, after all.

"Do you really think there's treasure on this garbage scow?" Jack asked.

"Don't let appearances fool you," Ray cautioned.

"He's right," I agreed. "If you want to hide treasure, you don't put it on a ship that looks like it *could* have treasure."

"I get it," Jack said. "It's sort of like when you want to kill somebody, you smile as you walk toward them."

"Exactly," Ray said. "Not that I'd know anything about killing anybody, but it's classic misdirection, something both magicians and pickpockets do. Speaking of which ..."

He held out his hand ... which was holding my watch!

Jack started to laugh and then stopped himself. He looked at his own bare wrist.

Ray was now holding Jack's watch, too.

He handed us back our watches—just as the soldier who was leading us stopped, and we bumped into him. "Here it is, General, sir!" he yelled as he snapped to attention and saluted.

"Yeah, good ... thanks," Ray mumbled in a not very general-like manner.

We walked into the cabin and Ray closed the door behind us.

"This is different," Jack said.

"Is it ever!" I agreed.

We had left behind the garbage scow and were now on a luxury liner—or at least what I figured one would look like. There were carpets on the floor, and expensive furniture, and paintings on the walls, and in the corner was a full-sized grand piano, similar to the one in the lobby of The Princess.

"The occupant of this cabin is an aristocrat—I think he's related somehow to Spanish royalty—and he wanted to travel in the manner to which he was accustomed," Ray explained. "Pretty fancy digs. Him being on this ship is one of the things that tipped off our agents in Barcelona."

"Always look for what doesn't fit," I said.

"Always," Ray agreed.

"Has this cabin been searched?" I asked.

"Completely. Everything except the safe."

I looked around. "I don't see a safe."

Ray walked over and, with one hand, swung a huge picture away from the wall, revealing a big wall safe hidden behind it.

"Nice safe. Fairly complicated, expensive and difficult to crack. That's good."

"How is that good?" I asked.

"Nobody has a safe like this installed on a ship unless there's something in there worth stealing," he explained.

That made sense. "Can you open it?" Jack asked.

"Actually that's why I brought George along. He's going to open it."

"Me?" I exclaimed, and Ray burst into laughter——he was obviously joking.

"I could teach you, but not today. It's a little tricky, and we don't have a lot of time."

Ray pulled a stethoscope out of his pocket and placed it around his neck.

"Are you going to pretend to be a doctor now?" Jack asked.

"Not today … although I have on occasion pretended to be a doctor. It's amazing how people take orders from a doctor or just let him into places. I remember this one time, in London, it was——"

"What do you need the stethoscope for?" I asked, cutting him off. I knew that once Ray went off on a story, it could be a long time before we got him back.

"I need this to listen to the safe."

He put the earpieces in his ears and then placed the other part against the safe. He started slowly turning the tumbler dial.

"Can you really——?"

"Ssshhhh!" Ray hissed.

"Sorry," Jack whispered.

Ray went back to concentrating on the safe. I took Jack by the arm and moved us toward the far end of the cabin. Slowly, quietly, we sat down on two of the soft leather chairs. With nothing else to do, I looked at the room.

In the far corner was a large, solid, wooden desk. The wood was reddish and gleamed in the light coming in through the porthole. It was made of the same wood as the grand piano. A big leather chesterfield matched the chairs Jack and I were sitting on. There were fancy lamps, and hanging from the ceiling was a crystal chandelier. It was easy to believe that the occupant of this room was royalty. The room seemed more suited to a palace than a broken-down ship. The closest thing I'd ever seen to this cabin was, of course, at The Princess Hotel, but even that didn't quite live up to these standards.

"There, got it!" Ray sang out.

He pushed down the handle of the safe and then pulled open the door. Jack and I jumped out of the chairs and rushed over.

"Hold this," Ray said. He had pulled out a painting and handed it to Jack. "Do you recognize it?"

I looked at the painting. "It does look familiar ... I guess," Jack said.

"You might recognize the artist. It's a Gauguin."

"I don't know that name," I replied.

Ray snorted. "And here's one for you," he said as he handed a second painting to me. It was smaller and darker—a portrait of a woman.

"Then you might have heard of this painter ... his name was Rembrandt."

"Yeah, right. Who is it really by?" I asked.

"Rembrandt."

"I'm holding a Rembrandt?" I gasped.

"One of his smaller pieces. You ever wonder what a million dollars looks like?" Ray asked.

"I can't even imagine that much ... wait ... are you saying this painting is worth a million dollars?"

"*Easily*."

He pulled out another painting. "This is a Picasso." He set it down on the floor. "And this is a Monet ... and a second Picasso." He pulled out both paintings.

"How much are these worth all together?" Jack asked.

"Enough money for the three of us to live like kings for the rest of our lives. Finding something of this value is like a dream come true for a safecracker, but of course it could never happen in the real world."

"Why not?" Jack asked.

"These pieces would be under the highest security imaginable, with guards, in museums. It's only because the Nazis already stole them and were going to sell them that a bloke like me even has a *chance* to steal them. My hands are sweating just being around them."

I suddenly thought about the sweat from my hands getting on the Rembrandt. I made sure I was holding it by the simple wooden frame.

"Might be a good thing that you boys are around, so I'm not tempted to skip off with these myself," Ray said. "I'm surprised ... I thought there might be more of them," he said, looking inside the safe.

"There's nothing else in there?" Jack asked.

"Oh, there are other things but nothing else I can take." He reached in and brought out a thick stack of money! "This is probably being used to finance some purchases for the Nazi cause, but I can't prove it so I can't take it."

He closed the door of the safe, pulled up the handle and then spun the dial.

"But you can take these?" I asked.

"That's why we're here."

"But won't that Spanish guy object, or protest or ... or ..."

"Call the police?" Ray asked, and then he chuckled. "He can't complain because if he did, then we'd have to arrest *him*."

"What?"

"It's simple. He can't protest our taking the paintings because then he'd have to explain why he had them in the first place, since we all know they were pilfered by the Nazis."

"I get it," Jack said. "He can't complain about you stealing them because they're already stolen!"

"Exactly!" Ray turned to me. "He catches on fast. Now, since our work is done, we should go before you two get into trouble for not doing your chores. Just leave the paintings. I'll make sure they're taken off the ship."

I put down the Rembrandt, leaning it carefully against the leg of the desk. I looked at it one last time. It was pretty, but how could it possibly be worth that much money? What made it worth more than the paintings hanging on the walls of this cabin? Actually the paintings on the walls were pretty ugly. I don't know much about art, but they didn't seem to fit with the rest of the room. Instead of being fancy and elegant, they were almost cheap ... wait ... wait.

"Ray, did you really think there would be more paintings on board?" I asked.

"The report indicated that there could be up to ten pieces, but reports are sometimes wrong."

"But that report, was it right about everything else?" I asked.

"Pretty well. The name of the ship, the passenger's identity, the location of the safe," he said.

I walked over and stood in front of one of the paintings. It was an ugly oil painting of a man fighting a bull. It almost looked like one of those paint-by-number kits.

"I was just wondering about this painting," I said, gesturing to the wall. "And that one, and that one. These paintings are bad."

"I think even Rembrandt's children could have done a better job than those," Jack joked.

"Exactly," I said. "There's something about them that's not right."

"Almost everything about them isn't right," Jack joked. "Guy must have been drunk that day or——"

He suddenly stopped himself mid-sentence. His expression changed. Jack walked over to the painting directly in front of me, took it off the wall and laid it down on the desk. He ran his fingers along the edge of the painting and then took a small knife out of his pocket.

"What are you doing?" Ray demanded.

"I think that maybe there's something hidden behind——"

"I gathered that, but you can't be hacking away at it with a pocket knife. Here."

Ray took the painting out of its frame and then removed a pair of tweezers from his pocket. He used them to carefully pull up a corner of the canvas at the back, and then, with his fingers, he started peeling back the canvas. As he moved to the front and lifted the top canvas, a hidden oil painting was revealed! The face of a woman emerged from beneath the bullfighter, and this painting had the same dark colours of the Rembrandt.

"Wow," said Ray. "I guess it was your turn to teach me a magic trick. And that one's a whole lot better than pulling a rabbit out of your hat!"

CHAPTER NINETEEN

"UNBELIEVABLE," the commander said. He was our father's boss—technically the boss of all operations at the hotel when Little Bill wasn't there.

"Quite the haul," Ray agreed.

We were sitting in the office of the commander—along with our parents. I was a little nervous. I'd seen him around but never said more than "hello, sir" as I passed him in the halls of the hotel. It wasn't like he had much to do with the floor cleaning. I wasn't really sure why we were all there, except that Ray had told the commander how much we'd helped, and now Ray said he was dead set and determined to get some official permission to, as he said it, "put our God-given talents to work." And for that we would need the commander's okay as well as our parents'. I had a feeling I knew which was going to be harder to get.

Around us, either leaning against the walls or laying on the tables, were the pieces of art that had been confiscated from the ship: the five pieces found in the safe and five more discovered underneath other paintings in the cabin.

"What is your estimate of the total value of the paintings?" he asked Ray.

"Could be anywhere up to four million dollars," Ray replied.

Jack let out a whistle.

"Do you realize that there aren't more than a dozen museums in the whole world that have more valuable art than we have in this room?" the commander said. "Ten masterpieces."

"And we would have only had five if it weren't for the boys here," Ray said.

"This was a great discovery," the commander said. "My reports show that the cabin had already been searched and declared clean. You boys saw what others missed, and if you hadn't been there, those paintings would have sailed off the same way they sailed in. You have struck a valuable blow against the Nazis." He turned to my parents. "You must be very proud of your boys."

"We are," our father said.

"Yes, of course we are, but I still want to know why my boys were even there," our mother said.

"That's where I have to apologize," Ray said. "It was all my idea."

"Just because you had an idea doesn't excuse their decision to go with you. They both knew they were not to leave the hotel," she said.

"We didn't go very far," Jack said. "We never really lost *sight* of the hotel."

"And we did finish our jobs," I added. As soon as we'd gotten back, we'd made doubly sure that we completed our tasks. Jack finished mopping the ballroom and put all the tables and chairs back in place, and I emptied the garbage cans in all the rooms.

"They weren't in any danger," Ray said. "They were perfectly safe. It wasn't like they were out on some mission in the middle of the night on the streets of Hamilton."

"There were soldiers and guards and agents all around us," I added, to support what Ray was saying.

"Nevertheless you should have asked permission," my mother said. "Either from the commander or from one of us. We never agreed to you boys getting involved in anything riskier than cleaning and chores."

"To tell you the truth," Ray said, "I think it's almost a crime to have these boys here mopping and sweeping and emptying rubbish bins. It's like hitching a couple of race-horses to a milk wagon and then being upset when they start pulling hard on the reins and chomping at the bit."

"They are *not* going out on missions," my mother said.

"I agree. They're just boys," my father added.

"That's where you're wrong," Ray replied. "George there can pick a lock better than almost any man I know."

Both parents looked at me in shock.

"He took to it like an otter to water," Ray explained. "I hardly had to show him."

"What else have you been showing him?" my mother demanded.

"Hardly anything that—"

"Why are you showing them anything?" she asked.

"Just trying to give them an education."

"An education is what they get in school!" our mother snapped.

The room got very silent and uncomfortable. I wished that Little Bill were here because he would have known what to say to ease the tension.

"I know they're your children," Ray finally said to break the silence. "And I know that it's maybe not my place … but still … just think about it." Ray stood up. "You've done a good job with these boys," he said.

"Thank you," my mother replied. "And we're not angry with you … really."

"As long as you're not angry with your boys." He turned to the commander. "Just think about what I said … just think before you decide."

The commander looked like a man with a lot on his mind, not all of it having to do with a couple of kids who may or may not have been too talented to take out the trash. "Boys, please wait outside my office," he said.

We both got to our feet.

"And, Ray, you are also dismissed."

Ray shook hands with the commander and my parents and then came out with us, closing the door behind him. We walked over, and Jack and I sat down on the chesterfield, but Ray stood right over top of us.

"It got a little frosty in there," he said.

"It was downright chilly," I replied.

"Commander's been a bit out of sorts lately. Not sure why, but I have the feeling that something's about to happen ... something big."

"How do you know?"

"I hear things, I listen, I look. You know they're going to cancel all leaves for the guards this Saturday."

"Are you sure? Dad didn't mention that to us," I said.

"And he'd know," Jack said.

"I'm sure he does know. It hasn't been passed on to anybody just yet."

"But you know."

"I know lots of things I'm not supposed to know," Ray replied and then gave a little wink.

"So there's something big happening this weekend," Jack said.

"Something, yes. Big, yes. But I'm not sure what. The thing I can't figure is why they want all the guards. It's almost like they think that there's ..."

Ray let his sentence trail off but we all had the same thought—like there was going to be an attack on the hotel.

I'd started to say that very thing when the door to the office opened and the commander appeared, followed by our mother and father.

"With the agreement of your parents, we will consider allowing you boys to become involved in something more sensitive at the hotel," the commander said.

"That's great!" I said, jumping to my feet.

"But ..." the commander continued.

I hated *buts*.

"But those tasks will only commence upon further discussion with, and agreement from, higher authorities."

Of course I knew he was talking about Little Bill.

"And until that agreement is forthcoming, you will be denied access to The Princess Hotel," the commander said.

"We can't come here at all?" I asked.

The commander nodded his head.

"That ain't fair!" Ray said. "It's like they're being punished for something that I did."

"They aren't being punished," the commander said. "And this whole situation will be resolved within the week. It's more like a one-week holiday."

Jack looked at me and I knew what he was thinking, the same way he knew what I was thinking.

"So we can come back on Monday?" Jack asked.

"No guarantees, but that certainly seems to fit the proposed timeline."

"Until then, you are not to come within *sight* of the hotel," my father said. "And if you fail to follow that order, I can guarantee that you will never come here again. Understand?"

"Yes, sir," Jack said, and I nodded in agreement.

We both knew that this had less to do with reassigning us than with keeping us away until after Saturday. I didn't know what was going to happen, but I now had a pretty good idea where and possibly when.

CHAPTER TWENTY

I SHIFTED ALONG, keeping pace, as the opposing team used a series of lateral passes to move the ball across the rugby field. Each time, they lost a few yards in the toss and gained it back in the run, only to be met by a wall of our defenders. There wasn't much time left in the game—there *couldn't* be much time left—and all we had to do was hold them off and we'd win. We were up by four points, so unless they got a try, they couldn't catch us.

Suddenly there was a shift and one of their players burst through, shedding defenders and making for the far side of the field. I angled toward him, trying to make sure he didn't get by me on the far side but not overplaying him so that he could cut back and go under me. He was big and getting bigger as he closed the distance between us. He was also fast, and there was no hope of anybody catching him from behind. It was me or nobody. He thundered forward—he was trying for the outside—then all at once he changed direction, heading right at me, a straight arm out to bowl me out of the way!

His fist slammed against my chest, pushing me back, and I reached up and grabbed him, wrapping my arms around his middle. He kept running, his legs pumping furiously, pounding into me as he used his free hand to punch me in the face! I dug my fingers into his back and my legs got tangled up in his, and then I felt myself falling backward. It was like the whole thing was happening in slow motion. I wanted to push him away or twist to the side, but I couldn't—I wouldn't—do either. I clung to him and was only jolted back to real life and real time when his full weight crashed against my chest! My whole rib cage seemed to compress and air rushed out of my lungs—but I didn't let go.

I could feel the rugby ball trapped between our bodies— it felt like there was a rugby ball–sized crater in my chest. He tried to get the ball free so that one of his teammates could pick it up and continue the run, but I wasn't going to let him do that. I hung on to him with all my might, and the ref blew the play down ... no, he was blowing the whistle to signal that the game was over!

I released my grip and the player I had tackled got up. He reached down and offered me a hand.

"Good play, old chap," he said as he pulled me to my feet.

I tried to answer but I couldn't—I didn't have any air in my lungs. They felt like they had been deflated. I doubled over.

"Way to play, Georgie!" one of my teammates yelled as he slapped me on the back.

Almost instantly I was in the middle of a mob of players congratulating me and each other on our victory. I was happy—but I would have been happier if I could have drawn a full breath.

"Are you all right?" Jack asked.

I nodded my head. "Good ... had the wind ... knocked out ... of me," I panted. "Better ... now."

Slowly I joined the team as we assembled in the middle, offered three cheers for the opposition and then formed a line to shake hands with them.

"That was a game saver," one of them offered as he shook my hand.

"Good game, good tackle," a second player said.

"You showed real heart out there," another player added.

I looked up. He was the guy I'd tackled.

"I almost showed guts and a lung, too," I said.

He chuckled and slapped me on the back. Having him congratulate me wasn't surprising. Rugby was like that. One minute the enemy was trying to take off your head, and the second the whistle sounded, everybody was your buddy again.

The fans—and it seemed like every student from both schools was there—cheered as we left the field. I trailed behind slowly. It wasn't just that I was having trouble drawing a full breath but my left leg was hurting and I was limping.

There was a loud whistle—like a bird call. I looked in the direction it came from, at the end of the field, and saw a priest standing there. Was he motioning for me to come over? Why would a priest want— Ray ... it had to be Ray.

I headed over and wasn't halfway there when I could clearly see it *was* Ray. He was standing in the shadow of some trees, well away from anybody else.

"What are you doing here?" I asked.

"Even a man of the cloth can appreciate a good rugby game." He spoke with a thick, rich Irish accent instead of his usual English accent.

"Why are you talking like that?" I asked.

"It always seems to me that priests should be Irish."

"But you're not Irish."

"And I'm not a priest, my son, but I can pretend to be both."

I guess that made sense. "Is there another reason you're here besides to watch a rugby game?"

"If God is everywhere, why wouldn't this be a fine place for one of his servants to be?"

"If God is everywhere, why are you here, specifically in this spot?" I wasn't letting this go.

"I heard something that might be of interest."

"I'm listening."

"What we'd talked about ... something happening at The Princess."

"Yes."

"It's definitely going to happen this Saturday. I heard it from three different sources."

"Intercepted mail?"

"Mail *and* radio transmissions."

"Do you know *what's* going to happen?" I asked.

"I'm not sure. I'm a priest ... only God knows everything ... and I don't mean Billy Stephenson. This time even *he* doesn't know."

"Do you have any idea what it might——?"

"Hello, George."

I spun around——it was Louise.

"Yeah ... hello."

"My apologies for interrupting ... please excuse me."

"No need to apologize," Ray said, his Irish accent so thick it almost dripped from his mouth. "I'm Father O'Sullivan ... and you are?"

"I'm Louise, Father," she said.

"Pleased to meet you," Ray sang out.

"It's my great pleasure, Father. Again, I'm sorry to disturb your conversation. I was just wondering, George, would you tell your brother that I have to leave? Please congratulate him for me."

"Sure ... of course."

"Thank you. So nice to meet you, Father ... goodbye, George."

Ray dipped his head slightly, and I waved goodbye as she left, leaving us alone again.

"I had no idea she was here," Ray whispered—his Irish accent was gone.

"Louise? How do you know Louise?"

"Do you know who she is?" Ray asked.

"Yeah ... she's Louise. She's Jack's girlfriend."

"She's a lot more than Jack's girlfriend!" Ray exclaimed.

"You know her?"

Ray laughed. "A lot of people in England would know her ... well, at least recognize her. It's not like she and I move in the same social circles."

"So who is she?"

Ray opened his mouth to speak and then stopped. "Maybe I've said too much all ready."

"Come on, Ray, tell me!"

"If you don't know, it's maybe better if I keep me mouth shut."

"I know she's somebody," I said. "Jack knows ... he just hasn't told me."

"And maybe I should follow his lead. I gotta run. I'll see you next week ... I'm sure they'll let you back in after this weekend."

"Wait!" I said as I grabbed him by the arm and stopped him from leaving.

"Easy on the priestly vestments, my son," he said—the Irish accent had returned.

"But tell me ... do you have any idea what's going to happen at The Princess?"

"Not sure, but the message said something about capturing The Princess and 'neutralizing the target.'"

"They're going to take over the hotel!" I gasped.

"Of course not. The way she's defended, they'd have to land a battalion of men, and there's no way they could do that."

"Why not?" I demanded.

"The only enemy vessel that could get close enough would be a U-boat, and it couldn't hold more than ten or twenty men ... not nearly enough to make a serious attempt to capture the hotel."

"So if they can't capture it, are they going to try to destroy it?" I asked.

"That would be my guess. And there's the rub. Nobody is sure, but they're taking no chances. There'll be enough soldiers pulled from around the island that it would take more than a battalion. Don't worry, your father will be safe. I gotta go."

He started off and then stopped and turned back to me. "And you have to keep this under your hat ... on the down low ... you can't let anybody know that old Ray told you anything."

CHAPTER TWENTY-ONE

"ARE YOU NOT FEELING WELL, George?" my mother asked.

"I'm fine … I feel good … why?"

"You've hardly touched your breakfast," she said, pointing down at my plate. "You've just sort of rearranged your eggs and sausage."

"I guess I'm not hungry. Dad hasn't eaten much of his."

We all looked at my father's plate. He hadn't touched his toast, had left part of an egg and his sausage was only half eaten.

He looked embarrassed. "I guess I'm not that hungry, either."

It was Saturday morning, and it looked as though I wasn't the only person nervous about what today was going to bring. But Jack was still pretty much in the dark—I'd kept my word to Ray and hadn't told him.

I felt bad keeping it to myself, but I would have felt worse breaking Ray's trust.

"I'd better get moving," Dad said as he got up from the table.

"And I should, too," Mom added.

"Where are you going?" I had a rush of fear that I already knew the answer.

"To work, of course," she replied.

I felt as if I'd been kicked in the stomach. She couldn't go to the hotel today. She *couldn't*!

"You can't go!" I blurted out.

She stopped. "Why not?"

Everybody was staring at me. What was I going to say?

"I lied," I said. "I'm really not feeling so good." That was hardly a lie—I did feel awful about her, and my father, being in danger.

"I thought so." She came over and put her hand against my forehead. "You don't feel hot ... not that that means anything. Is it your head or your stomach that hurts?"

"My stomach. That's why I didn't want to eat." I tried to look sick and pathetic at the same time. "Could you stay home and take care of me ... please?"

"I wish I could," she said, "but I really do have to go to work today. I wish I didn't."

She looked genuinely upset. Maybe I needed to push her just a little harder.

"But I'm sick," I said, trying to sound weak and whiny. "I shouldn't be alone."

"And you won't be," she said.

I started to smile but pushed it back into my sad, sick look.

"Jack," our mother said, "you need to stay here today with George."

"But I have plans!" he protested. "Louise and I are going to the beach and——"

"You'll have to cancel those plans, sport," our father said. "Your mother and I have to go to work, and that leaves you."

"But … but … but …" he sputtered. Jack stopped himself. He knew better than to argue.

"We really appreciate you doing this, Jack," our mother said.

"I guess I'll just go and see her this evening, when you get home," Jack muttered.

"That could be a problem. From what I've heard, if I'm not home by five or six, it could be late … very late," our father said

I wanted to say something, but what could I say? Mom reached over and gave my hand a little squeeze. "And you, mister, are going straight to bed."

I lay there thinking about my choices. I could tell Jack what Ray had told me. Of course, he'd be mad that

I hadn't told him earlier, and he'd be worried about Mom, and angry at me for letting her walk out the door when I knew something bad was about to happen.

Or I could just keep my mouth shut and pray that everything was going to work out. That would be the easiest thing—but not the right thing.

Slowly I got up and made my way to the kitchen, where Jack was doing the dishes.

"Jack?"

He turned around. He didn't look too happy, and I wasn't going to make him any happier.

"I have to tell you something ... actually lots of things."

"Go back to bed."

"I don't need to go to bed." I paused. "I'm not really sick."

"What?"

I took a deep breath. "I'm not sick. I was just saying that so——"

Jack practically leaped across the kitchen. He grabbed me by the shirt, lifting me right off my feet. "So that I couldn't see Louise and had to stay here and babysit you?" he demanded.

"No! I didn't know that was going to happen! My idea was to keep Mom from going to work today!"

"Why wouldn't you ... wait, is it happening today?" he asked.

I nodded my head and he slowly lowered me to the floor.

"How do you know?"

"Ray told me, yesterday, after the rugby game, when you went into the locker room."

"Why didn't you didn't tell me?" he demanded.

"Ray made me promise. Besides, what difference would it make if I *had* told you?"

"I don't know. What did he say … what *exactly* did he say?" Jack asked.

"He told me that they didn't know a lot of details, but it was going to happen this Saturday. He said the operation was aimed to either capture or neutralize The Princess."

"Neutralize? What does that mean?"

"I don't really know … maybe it means that they're going to bomb it or burn it down or … I don't know."

"And both our parents are there," Jack said.

I nodded my head. "Dad will take care of Mom."

"I know he'll try. I just wish there was something we could do. Maybe we could go to the hotel or—"

"We can't go to the hotel," I said, cutting him off. "And what good would it do if we did? Ray told me they brought in extra guards from all over the island. He said it was going to be the safest place on the island."

"Yeah, right. If it's so safe, why did you try to stop Mom from going there?" Jack asked.

"I wanted her to be here, where nobody is trying to do anything."

"Right, and that didn't work. So if she's there, and Dad's there ... are we just going to sit around here at home and wait?"

I couldn't really imagine what we could do to make a difference ... but Jack was right. Sitting at home twiddling our thumbs wasn't going to help anybody, and we'd probably go crazy trying to sit still.

"I figure nothing's going to happen till tonight. If they're bringing men in by U-boat, they'll have to wait till it's good and dark," I said.

"Right," said Jack. "So we hang out here like good little boys till it gets late, and then we scope out the hotel."

"And if somebody tries to stop us?"

"Nobody's gonna stop us, little brother," Jack said, "because nobody's gonna see us. We're good at this spy stuff, remember?"

"Well, a guy's gotta do what he does best!" I answered with a grin.

I looked at my watch for the two-thousandth time. It was almost six and the sun was setting. We sat on the porch and waited as the light started to fade. The day was over but the night was just beginning.

Jack and I had already changed into our black clothes and muddied up our shoes. This was one night we really didn't want to be seen. Jack's knee was twitching like crazy, like it always did when he was restless. I was trying to stay very, very calm.

"Do you think we'd hear if something happened?" I asked.

"If there was an explosion or something, maybe we would hear," Jack said. "But it's still pretty early ... well, early if something is going to happen after dark."

"That's the only time it would happen," I said. I shook my head. "I'm sorry I didn't tell you yesterday. And I'm glad you're here."

"Nothing personal, but I think I would have rather spent the day with Louise than you."

"You really do like her, don't you?"

"Are you just figuring that out?" Jack asked. "She really is special."

"Ray thought so, too."

"Ray knows her?"

"He met her yesterday when he was talking to me. He said he didn't know her but that he recognized her," I said.

"That doesn't surprise me," Jack said. "He is English."

"So are millions of people and I don't think they *all* recognize each other."

"Not all, but lots of them would recognize her because ..." Jack stopped.

"Because why?"

"I can't tell you," Jack said.

"I told *you* everything. I think you should tell me everything, too. No secrets."

He didn't answer right away. "Maybe it's okay. A lot of the kids at school already know. But if I tell, you have to promise that—"

"I won't tell anybody, promise."

"Okay," he said. "The reason Ray would know her is because she's very important. Her family is very important. In fact, the *most* important family."

"What does that mean?"

"You've heard of the king and queen," Jack said.

"Of course I've heard of ... you're saying that she's royalty?"

Jack nodded. "But you can't tell anybody," he said.

"I won't," I promised. "I gave you my word. I just can't get over the fact that my brother is dating royalty."

"Yeah, she's like a princess."

I laughed. "Princess Louise, like the hotel."

"Well, Louise is named after the princess that the hotel was named after."

"That's a strange coincidence that the hotel and she are both ..."

I let the sentence trail off. Jack's shocked look made me realize that he and I were thinking the same thing. What if all those reports weren't about agents taking over The Princess Louise Hotel? What if the real target tonight was Princess Louise ... the girl?

CHAPTER TWENTY-TWO

"YOU SHOULDN'T JOKE around about that," Jack said.

"Joke around about what?" I asked, trying to act innocent.

"That they might be coming after Louise instead of the hotel."

"I didn't say anything about Louise," I said.

"But you implied it."

"I didn't imply anything. You were just thinking the same thing I was."

"Don't tell me I'm getting as crazy as you, seeing spies behind every door and agents everywhere, imagining everybody is in danger."

"I don't think that there are spies everywhere," I said. "And I don't think that everybody is in danger ... not *everybody*."

"Just stop it, right now!" Jack snapped. "Louise isn't in danger ... it's the hotel ... The Princess Louise Hotel, not the real Princess Louise."

"I'm sure you're right," I said. Actually I wasn't sure, but I knew I couldn't argue with him right now or he'd just dig in his heels. There might not be time for either a fight or a discussion.

Jack seemed to relax as I didn't press him on it. Without me arguing with him, he was left with the argument going on in his head.

"Tell me again what Ray said about the hotel," Jack finally asked.

"He said they were going to either capture or neutralize it, but he didn't see any way the Nazis could possibly land enough men to capture it."

"But it wouldn't take that many men to neutralize it. Just a couple of men with a couple of bombs could do that," Jack said.

"If it *is* the hotel."

I knew it was risky to throw in that part, but he didn't jump down my throat. There was a long pause. What was he thinking of right now?

"And if it was a person?" Jack asked. "What would it mean to neutralize somebody?"

"If they couldn't capture the person, then they would kill him," I answered, careful not to say "her" or "Louise."

"Well then ... we have to *do* something!" Jack said. "We have to save her and——"

"We don't even know if it has anything to do with her."

"What?" Jack demanded. "First you try to convince me she's in danger, and now that I'm convinced, you're trying to talk me out of it? You can't have it both ways!" he snapped. "We have to get to the hotel—now—so we can get some help, some soldiers, tell Dad!"

"Sure, but think about it. We get to the hotel—where we're not supposed to be, by the way—and if we're lucky and they don't march us straight home again, we get our chance to tell somebody what we think is about to happen. And what are the odds that they're going to believe us? As far as everybody but Little Bill knows, we're just a couple of dumb kids from Canada."

"I don't care about that. I just care about Louise. We need to make sure she's safe. We have to go, right now. We don't have time to waste—the sun is almost down."

"You're right, we have to do something," I said. "And we have to go right now."

"Good. If we hurry, we can get to the hotel and—"

"No, not to the hotel," I said. "We're going to Louise's house. We know there will be tons of people at the hotel already, so if that's where the trouble happens, it'll be okay. Our job is to keep an eye on Louise's house. If our guess is wrong ... well, no big deal."

"And if we're right?"

"If we're right, then we run and get help ... fast."

I expected Jack to argue, but he didn't.

"Okay, we'll do what you say... but we can't stay there all night. When Mom and Dad finally get home and find us gone, they'll *kill* us."

"We'll leave them a note and say I felt better and we're both sleeping over at Jerome's house tonight." Jerome was a friend from school, and Jack and I had slept over at his place before.

"That might work. You write the note and I'll be right back," Jack said.

I went to the kitchen drawer and rummaged for a piece of paper and a pen or pencil. I found a clean sheet and a pencil and started to write the note.

"There," Jack said. "I'm ready to go."

I looked up. He was carrying one of Dad's service revolvers. I was a little shocked—but a lot reassured.

CHAPTER TWENTY-THREE

"WE'D GO FASTER if I could turn on the flashlight," I said.

"We'd go faster if you'd shut up and save your breath," Jack replied. "Keep the flashlight off. There's some light from the stars."

"I just wish it was a full moon instead of a new moon," I said.

"It wouldn't be happening today if there was a full moon," Jack pointed out. "Do you think it was coincidence that it was planned for tonight, when the sky is completely dark?"

Jack was right. The best time for a clandestine operation was at night, and the best night was when it was darkest, and that was during the new moon phase. This was the perfect night.

I tripped over a root and stumbled forward, catching myself before I fell on my face. Rather than travelling along the road, we were taking a path through the woods that would lead us to the beach. From there we'd go along the beach and up to Louise's home—the home she shared with her guardian, Mrs. Farrow.

We hit the beach. It was flat, and the water reflected some of the limited starlight, making the way easier, the travel faster.

"This probably means nothing," Jack said.

"I know."

"At the end of the night, probably nothing will have happened either at the hotel or with Louise."

"I know that, too ... but still, this is the right thing to do."

Louise and her guardian lived in a house high on a hill, just off the beach. It was set well apart from other houses. I'd never been in it, but Jack had pointed it out, and he said that he and Louise would often sit on the veranda, sipping lemonade and watching the ocean in the distance. I think he was just saying all that to make me jealous, but the lemonade was the only tempting part for me. Okay, being close to the beach would have been nice, too—at least normally. Now being close to the ocean just meant being close to where agents would be put ashore. They wouldn't have very far to go and there wouldn't be much time to intercept or stop them.

"I think this is the path up," Jack said as he came to a stop.

"You don't know?"

"Everything looks different in the dark. I'm pretty sure it's this path."

We started up and had gone only a few feet when Jack tripped and fell. I rushed forward to see if he was okay but stopped dead in my tracks when I realized what he had tripped over. It was a rubber raft, pulled to the side but still protruding onto the footpath.

Jack looked up at me. Even in the dim light I could see the look of fear in his eyes. We both knew this could mean only one thing.

"Is there only one raft?" I asked, breaking the silence.

He got to his feet. "I don't see any others."

"That means there aren't any more than four."

"There are three other rafts?" Jack asked.

"No, not rafts, people. This raft wouldn't hold more than four people. There can't be more than four of them who came ashore in this raft."

"That makes sense. Four came ashore. I'm going to make sure that none leave the shore."

Jack pulled something out of his pocket and I saw a glint of light—he was holding his knife. He plunged it into the raft and it started deflating with a loud hissing—way too loud! How far would the sound travel? He plunged the knife into the raft again and again, and with each thrust, the noise was less. The entire raft collapsed into a flat, black shadow on the ground.

Jack rolled it into a thick bundle and lifted it. "I'm going to toss it into the woods so they'll waste time looking for it."

"Wait!" I said, grabbing him by the arm. "*We're* wasting time. We have to go and get help."

"The hotel is at least thirty minutes from here no matter how fast you run. What if we don't have thirty minutes? What if they're coming back right now? Why would they wait around? They'd get in and out."

That thought sent a shudder up my spine because it made perfect sense. They could be coming back down right now.

"Let's get off the path," Jack said.

I followed him into the thick brush. As we pushed our way through some bushes, the thorns dug into my legs. Jack threw the corpse of the raft underneath a bush. It was practically invisible even though I was looking right at it.

"We'll go up to the house," Jack said.

"I think one of us should go to the hotel right away and—"

"The fastest, most direct way to the hotel is right up this path. We'll pass by and have a look so we know more, and then we'll make a decision."

I was pretty sure I knew what decision was right, but I wasn't going to argue with Jack. That was useless and would just waste whatever time we had. He went back down to the path and I followed right behind, almost tripping over him.

He stopped. "I want you to hang back—at least fifty feet."

"I think we should stay together."

"And I don't think we should. If they've left somebody on the path as a sentry, we wouldn't want him to get us both. Better if it's only one—that way the other can still go for help."

"Okay ... sure ... that makes sense," I agreed. There was also something else that made sense, but I didn't really like where the logic led. "If one of us should hang back, it should be you."

"Me?"

"Yeah. If somebody stops me, they'll be less worried because I'm just a kid. Maybe I can bluff my way out of it. Besides, if I get caught, I'm going to need somebody to rescue me, and you're the one with the gun."

I almost hoped Jack would argue and insist on going first. He didn't.

"Okay, you lead. Her house is straight ahead about two hundred feet. There's a stand of bush at the end of the trail. Stop right there and wait for me. And if you see something, yell ... if you can."

"Believe me, if I stumble into somebody, I'm going to yell so loud that they'll be able to hear me at the hotel."

I started up the path. I held the flashlight but I no longer had any desire to turn it on. The dark was my best defence. I felt the flashlight's weight, wondering what would happen if I brought it down on the side of somebody's head. It had a good heft to it. It could certainly dent a skull. I felt a surge of confidence as I wielded it like a club. Anybody who got in my way would get a good one right in the head. They'd think I was unarmed, and then *smack*—which made me feel better, until I realized that the people at the end of the path would be armed with Lugers and rifles. Somehow using a flashlight as a weapon wasn't so confidence inspiring any more.

I came to the top of the path and ducked behind the bushes. Louise's house was a short ways off, sitting on its own. The nearest neighbour wasn't within sight or sound ... well, within the sound of a gunshot but not close enough to hear a muffled scream or a door being bashed in. I looked at the front door. It seemed to be intact. The blackout curtains were down, although I could see a thin line of light at the side of one window. It all seemed so peaceful. Maybe nothing was wrong and they were just sitting inside playing cards or a board game. But what about the rubber raft? Maybe it belonged to somebody on the island—boy, would we be in trouble if we'd destroyed some innocent person's raft.

I looked back down the path and beyond—I could see, and hear, the ocean. I knew that this side of the island was protected by a set of reefs and that I was hearing waves hitting against the rocks. I caught sight of movement and made out Jack's silhouette closing in on me—I *hoped* it was Jack's silhouette.

"Jack!" I hissed.

He reacted instantly and dropped right beside me.

"Do you see anything?"

"Nothing unusual."

"We have to get a closer look."

Jack started to get up. I grabbed his shirt and kept him from rising.

"Unless you're going to knock on the front door, what do you expect to see?"

"I don't know. If we got closer, maybe I could listen at the window or try to peek in, or maybe I could go in through the door at the back that leads into the basement."

"You're not going into the house!" I snapped. "Look, how about if I take off and get help, and you stay here and watch, and if you need to, well, do whatever you have to."

Jack nodded. "Okay."

He'd agreed too easily. That made me nervous.

"Jack, you have to promise you're not going to go into the house, that you're not even going to go *up* to the house. Promise?"

He didn't answer.

"Look, unless you promise, I'm not going anywhere," I said.

"Like you could stop me if I wanted to go in there," he snorted.

"Maybe I couldn't, but I'd try. You really want to get in a wrestling match here in the dark, outside this house, right now?"

"George, just go and get—"

He stopped in mid-sentence. A light had appeared in the window overlooking the veranda. It was a red light, and it flashed on and then off and on and—

"It's Morse code," Jack said.

"I figured that," I said. "But do you know what it's saying?"

"I studied it in Boy Scouts ... you did, too. There are two dashes and two dots ... and another dot ... and dot, dot ... and I think that's a dash."

"Yeah, I saw that, but what does it mean?" I asked. "Look, it's repeating the same pattern."

"Okay," Jack said. "Two dashes and a couple of dots ... that's the letter ... um ..."

"Z," I said.

"Yeah, right, and then the one dot is *e*."

"Okay, *z-e* and then two more dots. That's an *i*."

"And the final dash, I know that's a *t*. So they're spelling '*z-e-i-t*.'"

"'*Z-e-i-t*'?" I questioned. "That's not even a word. Maybe we got one of the letters wrong, or we have them in the wrong order."

"Or you're thinking the wrong language. *Zeit* is German for time."

If there was a shred of doubt about what was going on, it had been destroyed.

"But why would they want to know the time?" I asked. "Don't they have a watch or—?"

I spun around to look out at the ocean. There, faint but unmistakable, were little dot-and-dash answers coming from a boat, telling them not the current time, but the time of the pickup.

"Do you see them?" I asked Jack.

"I see them. I'm trying to read them."

The light was faint and far away, and the dots and dashes sort of blurred together. I stared and then they stopped completely. They couldn't risk sending a long message—somebody on shore might detect them.

"I think they used the code for three and zero, in numerals," Jack said.

"Thirty. Does that mean they're leaving in thirty minutes for the pickup? Or that they'll be at the rendezvous spot in thirty minutes or—"

"I only saw the last part of the message, and they might have used any number before the thirty—which could be twelve-thirty or two-thirty in the morning. But that wouldn't make any sense. Why would they wait that long?"

"Maybe the tide is low and they can't get over the reefs until the middle of the night. If that's the case, then we have time to get help," I said.

"Is the tide low?"

I shook my head. "I don't know."

"Because if they were saying thirty minutes, then there's no time," Jack said. "I need you to stay here. I can't do it by myself. We need to work together."

I was afraid of that—and almost as afraid of the next possibility: that the two of us together *couldn't* do it.

CHAPTER TWENTY-FOUR

JACK CAME BACK up the path.

"Did you do it?" I asked.

"It's done. Let's go."

We travelled through the underbrush, circling the house so we could come at it from the back. While Jack had been down below on the path, I'd been watching the front of the house like my life depended on it. Which I guess it did. There had been no more signals, no more anything. The house sat in darkness, except for the little hints of light around the edges of the screens, and no sound came from within. Only the croaking of the tree frogs and the rumble of the ocean broke the silence. I often found the sound of the waves very calm and restful. Tonight it was unnerving, knowing the ocean was so close and what was lurking out there, but not knowing what role it was eventually going to play in the night's adventures.

We arrived at the very back of the house. It was completely dark—not even a sliver of light came from behind the blackout screens.

"Do you see the door?" Jack asked.

"I can't see anything. Are you sure there's even a door there?"

"I know it's there. Louise uses it when she sneaks out at night to meet me."

I looked at Jack and he smiled.

"After Mom and Dad have gone to bed and her guardian's asleep, we meet sometimes. I wait for her right by the door."

I wasn't sure what to say.

"It's not like we meet all the time," he said. "It was five or six times."

"Five or six?"

"Okay, six times."

"It didn't seem like the sort of thing you'd lose count of."

Jack led the way out of the underbrush and across a short open space. If anybody was looking out one of those darkened windows, we'd be seen. We pressed close to the house and I could now see the door. Jack took the handle and—

"It's locked," he hissed.

"Move," I said.

I reached into my pocket. There—as always—was my pick. It had almost become my good luck charm.

I held on to the handle with one hand and inserted the pick into the lock.

"Do you need light?" Jack whispered.

"Nope."

What I wanted to say—but didn't want to risk making noise or wasting time—was that you didn't use your eyes to pick a lock. It was all in your fingertips. In some ways it was actually easier to pick a lock in the dark. That was why Ray had told me to close my eyes if I was having trouble.

There was a click—it was unlocked. I turned the handle and swung the door open.

Jack stepped forward. He was holding the pistol. "Follow ... use the railing ... there are four steps down."

How would he know that? I thought Louise came out the door, so when did he ever go through it?

I held on to the railing and eased down, feeling each step with my toe before committing my foot.

"Close the door," Jack whispered.

I knew it was the right thing to do, but it meant closing off our escape route. Reluctantly I reached back and pushed the door until it silently kissed shut, sealing us in. Our plan was for Jack to go up the stairway to the main floor door and listen, maybe peek through the keyhole. If we could find out for sure if there were four of them, we'd at least know what we were facing.

"Stay here," Jack said.

I didn't need to be told twice. He started forward—a shadow silently moving in the darkness—and then he fell with a muffled thud. He got up and—

"George," he hissed.

Slowly I moved toward him and froze as a flashlight beam came on and— It was aimed at what Jack had tripped over. It was a woman, her eyes wide open and wild, all tied up and with a gag in her mouth and a bright, blood-red gash on her head! I recognized her. It was Louise's guardian, Mrs. Farrow!

The woman made a muffled sound through her gag as though she was trying to talk. Jack put a finger up to his lips to silence her. He handed me the flashlight, and I made sure the beam stayed down and close to her face but didn't shine directly into her eyes. Jack undid her gag.

"They have—"

Jack put his hand over her mouth. "Quietly," he whispered.

She nodded her head and he moved his hand. "They have—"

Again she was too loud and again he silenced her. "We know they have Louise," Jack whispered. "And they're still here ... right above our heads. You have to be quiet. Do you understand?"

She nodded and he removed his hand.

She took a deep breath. "Thank goodness you're here, Jack. I thought if anybody would come and find me here it would be you!"

"Me?"

"Who else would be sneaking in to see Louise?"

"You know about that?" he gasped.

"I know lots of things, but that's not important. You have to go and get help."

"There isn't time," Jack said. "We think they're going to leave soon. How many of them are there?"

"There are three, but one isn't doing so well," she said. "I stabbed him."

"You what?"

"I plunged a paring knife into his stomach. Did you think I was going to let them take Louise without a fight? That's when they slugged me. Please, could you untie me?"

"Oh, sorry. Sure." Jack said. He turned her around and worked at untying her hands. The knots must have been very tight because he was struggling. Finally her hands were freed.

"One of you must run for help," she repeated.

"We don't think there's going to be time," Jack said. "I want you to go and get help."

"I can't move nearly as fast as either of you two."

"But we can't leave. It'll take both of us to stop them."

"Do you really think the two of you can stop them?" she asked, with the tone of her voice leaving little doubt as what she thought of our chances.

"We have a gun," Jack said, showing her the pistol.

"There are three of them, they all have weapons and they're trained soldiers," she said, listing the reasons why we couldn't succeed.

"But they don't know about us," Jack said. "We have the element of surprise on our side."

"They're not going to be leaving the island," I said. "That's guaranteed. We destroyed their raft."

"Well played," she said. "But these men would be trained to fight to the death—they are prepared to die. They're not going to surrender." She paused. "Nor will they surrender Louise. They will kill her if they realize they're trapped."

"Then we just can't let them know."

"That means they will have to be killed. Do you really think you can shoot a man?" she asked.

"Yes," I said. "I *know* I can."

"Then you'll need more than that little peashooter between the two of you. Help me up."

Jack and I pulled her to her feet. She wobbled slightly, but we kept her upright. With our support, she slowly shuffled across the basement floor. She opened a door and the light of the flashlight shone on two rifles!

She grabbed one and handed it to Jack. Then she gave the second rifle to me. It was big and I was amazed at how heavy it was.

"They're loaded. Single shot, bolt action. It carries a real wallop. Have you boys ever shot a rifle?" she asked.

"Lots of times," Jack said. "We grew up on a farm."

"Good. I'm going to our neighbours and I'll send them to get help. Then I'm coming back. There are three of them so we need to even the odds." She chuckled. "Two boys and an old woman against three trained Nazi agents … seems about right."

CHAPTER TWENTY-FIVE

JACK LED THE WAY OUTSIDE, followed by Mrs.
Farrow, and I brought up the rear. I closed the basement
door behind us. The two of them had already covered the
short distance from the back of the house into the cover
of the underbrush. Nobody had seen them, or at least
nobody had shot at them, so I guessed it was safe for me.
I almost laughed at the thought of it being safe. Being at
home in my bed would have been safe. Nothing about this
was safe.

I slung the rifle over my shoulder and carefully made
my way across the open patch of ground. I tried to push
through the brush, but the rifle snagged on some branches
and I had to take it off my shoulder to move forward. Jack
and Mrs. Farrow were already retracing the route he and I
had travelled, circling the house and returning to the path,
the place we'd selected for our ambush.

I quickly caught up to them. I was keeping one eye on the ground, watching for roots, and the other on the house, so I wasn't moving very fast, but Mrs. Farrow was moving *very* slowly. She was old, and she had been smashed in the face and tied up, and she was obviously—understandably—distraught.

We stopped at the crest of the hill. Hidden in the bushes, we could see the house in one direction and the ocean in the other. I could feel the breeze coming off the water and hear the gentle rumbling of the waves. It was almost restful, almost peaceful.

"We're going to set up just down the path a bit," Jack said.

"My best route to get help is down the path and along the beach toward the school," Mrs. Farrow said. "The nearest house belongs to the Stricklands… it's less than a half mile. I'll be back as soon as I can."

"Look," Jack said, "we really appreciate you wanting to come back and help, but …"

"But I'm just an old woman," she said.

"Well …"

"I'm an old woman who served king and country in The Great War. I'll do whatever I need to do."

"She did take out that one agent," I said.

"And I'll take out the other two if I have an opportunity."

"Come back as soon as you can," Jack said. "Do they have a phone or a car?" he asked.

"Hardly anybody has a phone, and even fewer people have a car, but they do have a carriage and horses. I'll send Mr. Strickland off immediately and I'll come back and bring whoever I can to help."

"Wait at the bottom of the path," Jack said. "Do the Stricklands have a gun?"

"I don't know, but if they do, I'll bring it back."

"Good. Find a spot where you could fire at the Nazis as they cross the beach. We'll try to make sure they don't get that far, but—"

"Don't do anything if you don't have to," she warned. "Just wait. Let's hope that we can get help here before they try to leave."

"We'll wait as long as we can," Jack said. "We're not going to do anything to endanger Louise." He paused. "We'd better get into position."

Jack led the way down the path, holding on to Mrs. Farrow's hand to guide her. The path was fairly steep, plus somehow it seemed steeper going down than going up. Gravity had naturally slowed our climb, but now I had to work hard not to pick up speed.

"Okay, be careful," Jack said. "Here's the trip rope."

Jack stepped carefully over a piece of rope he'd taken from the rubber raft. He'd strung it across the trail, about six inches off the ground, pulled it tight and tied each end to a tree—perfect to trip somebody and send them tumbling down the trail head first. Or at least that was the plan.

"This is far enough. We'll wait for them here," Jack said.

"Please be careful, boys," Mrs. Farrow said.

"We will," I said.

"I am very fond of you, Jack," she said.

"Thanks."

"And so is Louise. Thank you for being here. I'd better be off."

She reached over, gave first Jack and then me a hug, and then set off down the path. She quickly vanished, caught up in the darkness, but we could still hear her footfalls and the crunch of loose gravel under her feet for some time after.

"We're going to hear them coming before we see them," I said.

"I'd like it if we were able to see them, too. You remember how well it worked when we were up in that tree outside the hotel?"

"Of course."

Jack pointed at a tree. "If you were up there, do you think you'd be high enough to see the house?"

"Only one way to find out. Gimme a boost."

We laid our rifles against the tree. He gave me a foothold with his hands and lifted me so I could grab the lowest branch. I pulled myself up and got my leg over the branch, hauling myself up until I was standing on the limb. The rest wasn't going to be nearly as hard. I pulled myself up from branch to branch. They were so close together that it felt more like walking up a set of stairs than climbing a tree. I climbed the tapering trunk of the tree until I wasn't sure it was safe to go any farther. I could feel the tree gently swaying in the breeze. I pushed aside a branch and peered through the leaves. I could see the outline of the house—the veranda, the windows facing toward the ocean, and most importantly, the front door.

"I can see it!" I said softly to Jack.

"Good. Let me know as soon as you see anybody coming," he replied, just as softly.

I had my arms wrapped around the trunk, but I let go with one arm so I could look at my watch. I brought my wrist right in front of my nose and turned it back and forth, trying to see the time in the little light that was available. It looked like it was almost eight-thirty. I tried to figure out how long it would take for Mrs. Farrow to reach the neighbours' home, for them get ready, travel to the hotel, and then finally for the soldiers to get back here. We couldn't hope for anything less than an hour—probably closer to ninety minutes. That meant that if we could stay put until then—if they would just stay inside the house until then—we'd have help, and we wouldn't have to try anything heroic ourselves.

Then, almost as though wishing had made the opposite come true, I saw the door of the house open and somebody came out.

I strained my eyes at the dark silhouette. Was it one person or two? Oh, it was one man helping another! The wounded man was being half carried, half supported. I waited for the third man and a glimpse of Louise to know that she was all right, but the door closed, blocking out the light from within. I waited for it to open again, but it didn't. Only the two were coming. Maybe they were leaving first because they couldn't move as fast. That meant that the other agent wouldn't be far behind them. They probably thought it was better to keep Louise inside until the wounded man was at the raft. That made sense, not to expose her any longer than necessary. I'd prayed they'd all stay inside, but at least now the odds had suddenly shifted in our favour. Two—one of them hurt—and then one was much more doable. No longer were we outnumbered.

I scampered down the tree, a branch whacking me in the face in my rush.

"Jack," I hissed as loud as I dared. "Two men ... one of them is the wounded man being helped."

"What about the third man? What about Louise?" Jack asked.

"Still inside ... probably giving these guys a head start."

"Okay ... this is good."

I started to ease down from the lowest branch.

"No, stay up there," Jack said. "Nobody is looking for you in a tree."

"My rifle, hand me my rifle."

Jack grabbed the rifle from where it leaned against the tree, started to lift it up and then hesitated.

"Too heavy, too awkward." He put it back down. "Take this." He removed the pistol from his waistband. He stretched up and I reached down as far as I could. He held it handle up, and I just managed to wrap my fingers around it and pull it up. It felt reassuring to have something to defend myself with.

I climbed back up the tree and stopped when I was about ten feet high, standing on a branch that was right over the path, the route they'd walk. This wasn't such a bad place to be, although maybe a foot or two higher would be even better. I stepped up onto the branch directly above me. More height and more foliage would hide any view of me from below.

I settled in and listened. There was no sound except the leaves rustling in the breeze and the ocean murmuring in the distance. I closed my eyes—maybe with one sense shut off, the others would work better. I turned my head, trying to focus my ears on the sounds. I heard nothing. They were coming down this path, weren't they? There wasn't another route that they could have taken, was there? They should have been here by now, or at least been close enough that I could hear them or— I heard loose gravel from up the path. They were coming. A double blast of relief and fear struck me.

I looked down, not for them but for Jack. He was invisible. Good. I knew where he was. He was just down the path, off to the right-hand side, rifle pointed at the spot where we hoped they'd land when they tripped over the rope. He would then jump forward and take them prisoner, hopefully without having to fire a shot. He *couldn't* fire a shot.

That was the weak point of them coming in two groups. The first two guys had to be captured or neutralized in silence so that the last man, the one with Louise, wouldn't know about the ambush.

The sound was getting louder. It wasn't so much footfalls as foot drags. It sounded like the injured man was being hauled down the slope, and that a small avalanche of dirt and stones was being pushed down before them. It was getting louder, and I could hear voices, but it wasn't words, it was moaning. That sent a chill up my spine.

A dark shape—two figures intertwined—came into view. A rush of stones preceded them, rolling right beneath my perch in the tree. The moaning got louder and there were German words that I could hear but didn't understand.

They were getting closer and closer and closer. There was no way they wouldn't hit the rope. As long as it held fast it would take out their feet. It would hold, wouldn't it? Thank goodness it was Jack who tied the rope, although maybe I should have checked on it myself just to be sure.

They weren't even trying to be quiet. I looked down through my feet as they passed underneath. The rope was only a few feet in front of them— They tumbled forward with a loud thud, and there was a muffled cry of pain as arms and legs and bodies hit the ground and slid forward!

"Don't move, or you're dead!" Jack said.

He was standing over top of the two men, and his rifle was aimed right at the head of the stronger man. Either they would listen or he would have to fire.

"Put your hands where I can see them," Jack said.

In the thin light I saw one of the men pull forward one hand and then the other. The second man didn't move. I didn't know if he *could* move. Jack had them! Now all we had to do was get them off the path, tied and gagged, before the third man appeared. We were two-thirds of the way.

"Do not move!" yelled a voice, and I practically fell from the tree.

Almost directly beneath me was the third man—and he had Louise! We had been so focused on the two men, we hadn't heard him coming down the path. In one hand he held a pistol aimed at Jack, and his other arm was around Louise's neck. I looked toward Jack. He still held the rifle on the men in front of him. Was he wondering if he could swing the rifle up and fire it? No, there was no way he could do it quickly enough—the man would shoot him. And even if Jack got off a shot, he might hit Louise.

"Do as you are told or you will die!" the man said. He was no longer yelling. He was speaking in perfect English with a German accent.

"If you shoot me, I shoot him," Jack said. He held firm.

"Then you will both be dead," the man replied. "He is a professional who is prepared to die for the Fatherland. Are you prepared to die?"

"If I need to," Jack said.

"Very gallant."

"Louise, are you all right?" Jack asked.

"I'm fine now that you're here."

"Aahhh, so there is a connection," the German said. "You are, as they say, her knight in shining armour, here to rescue the fair maiden. The true question is: are you prepared to have her die?"

He took the pistol and turned it toward Louise until it was right by her temple.

I saw Jack's hold on the gun falter ever so slightly. Was he going to give him the gun? If he did that, there was no going back, no hope for either Louise or him!

The man moved forward. He was inching toward the rope strung across the path. I knew that and Jack knew that. Just a couple more feet and— He stopped, right beneath my feet. I had the pistol in my hand. I could take a shot— No, his head and Louise's were too close together. I couldn't be any surer of hitting him than Jack could, and I couldn't risk shooting Louise.

"Okay, you win," Jack said as he lowered the rifle.

I knew what he was doing. He was offering the rifle, trying to lure the man closer, hoping he'd trip over the rope.

"Get his rifle!" the man called out, and the guy on the ground started to get up.

There was only one thing left to do. I jumped from the tree, leading with my feet and knees, and aimed right for the man, and Louise!

Time seemed to stand still as I flew through the air. I could see everything so clearly ... it was as if somebody had turned on a bright light. I saw the top of his head and his face—the expression of shock and surprise and fear— as he turned slightly around and looked up at the sound of tree branches springing back. And then he released Louise and turned completely around, raised and aimed his pistol in my direction, and there was a flash of light and an explosion!

CHAPTER TWENTY-SIX

"IT'S OKAY, I really don't need a wheelchair," I said.

"Whether or not you need it, you're still going to use one," the nurse said. "Regulations are regulations."

"But—"

"Don't argue with the nurse," my father said. "Never argue with a woman, because you're just going to lose in the end."

"Spoken like a good husband," she joked.

"The best," my mother added as she squeezed his arm.

The nurse helped me off the bed and into the chair. I slumped into it awkwardly, feeling a little light-headed. Maybe I needed the chair more than I wanted to admit.

"Now, the arm is doing very well," the nurse said. "And the gash to your head is healing nicely on the outside, but you're still going to feel the effects of that blow for weeks to come. I always knew rugby was a dangerous game."

The cover story was that I'd broken my arm and received a gash to the side of my head from the cleat of a rugby boot.

"It wasn't even a game," my father said. "He and his brother and a few other boys were just having a little scrimmage."

"I'm thinking he's played his last game," my mother said.

"But we've thought that before and been wrong," I said.

"Put your feet up," the nurse said as she started to wheel me away. My mother and father followed behind. "I must admit, we were all more than a little worried about that head injury," she said.

"His brother didn't think there was much up there to damage," my father joked.

"Where is Jack?" I asked.

"Waiting outside," my mother said.

"Well, whatever he had up there got scrambled," the nurse continued. "You certainly didn't make a lot of sense the day you came in. A lot of rambling on about spies and enemy agents and guns."

I still felt guilty for what I'd let slip in my semi-conscious state.

"Oh, you know how a boy's imagination works," my mother said.

"I only know from my brothers," she replied. "I have a daughter."

"I always wanted a daughter," my mother said. "It would have been so wonderful to dress a little girl in pretty dresses and fix her hair and—"

"I'll talk to Jack about that," I said, and all three of them laughed.

"Instead I live in a house with three men who think everything is a joke ... including a shot to the head."

A shot! She shouldn't have said that, because nobody was supposed to know about what really happened. Talking about guns was definitely off limits!

"Well, I guess from the other team's point of view, it was a pretty good shot to the head," my father agreed. "That kick almost separated him from his skull."

That was a good explanation. As far as almost everybody knew, my injury was the result of an unfortunate rugby accident. The only people who knew the truth—that my arm was broken jumping down from a tree and landing on a Nazi agent, and that the bullet from his Luger grazed my head—were the people at the hotel, and one doctor and one nurse here at the hospital.

My father opened the front door and the nurse wheeled me outside. It was a beautiful, sunny day, warm, but not too warm, with not a cloud in the sky. Jack was sitting on a bench just by the door. He waved and walked over.

"How you feeling, kid?" he asked.

"I've been better. I've been worse. Wait till Mom tells you about the new clothes she's going to buy you."

Jack looked confused, and everybody else started laughing. He didn't know what the laughter was about but was smart enough to know it was aimed at him.

"You try to keep your feet away from your brother's head," the nurse said. "He'll need some gentle care for the next while."

"I'll take care of him," Jack said. It sounded more like a threat than a promise.

"There's our car," my father said.

A big, black car with tinted windows was parked at the side of the hospital. It was really fancy. Fancier than anything I'd ever ridden in. Maybe fancier than anything I'd ever seen.

"Quite the snazzy ride," the nurse said.

"On leave from the hotel," my father answered. "I'll take it from here."

Before she could say a word, my father moved in behind my chair and wheeled me away from her.

"Thanks for everything," my mother said. "You've all been wonderful. Thank you."

"Here, give me your hand," Jack said.

He eased me up from the chair and my mother opened the back door. I lowered myself in and—— "Little Bill!" I exclaimed.

He was sitting in the back seat.

"So good to see you in your street clothes and not a hospital gown," Little Bill said. He gestured to the seat opposite him and I settled into it.

Next my mother climbed in, followed by my father and then Jack. Jack sat beside me and my parents beside Little Bill.

"Driver," Little Bill said, "please."

The engine started and the car began to move.

"This is not the first time we've met after a hospital stay," Little Bill said.

"But I hope it's the last," I replied.

After our first adventure at Camp X, I'd been knocked unconscious and woke up in a bed. That time I had to be told what had gone on. Not this time. I remembered everything. Me flying through the air; the searing, burning pain as the bullet grazed my skull; landing on the Nazi agent and knocking him forward; Jack taking all three men prisoner; Louise being frantic but free; help arriving; and finally, me being taken to the hospital to have my broken arm set and the wound on my head treated. The hardest part of the whole thing had been explaining it to our parents. Especially our mother.

"Louise sends her greetings," Little Bill said.

"You've talked to her!" Jack exclaimed.

"I met with her and her parents. They asked me to convey their profound gratitude for what you boys did."

"It was nothing," Jack said.

"No time for false modesty. It was remarkable. Louise was very sad that she didn't have an opportunity to say goodbye before she had to leave."

I knew how upset Jack had been as well.

"Better she's somewhere else, and safe," Jack said.

"Yes, her safety is the primary concern," Little Bill said. "And now she's back with her family."

"That is wonderful," my mother added. "I know how much she missed her parents."

"And they missed her," Little Bill said.

"I still can't believe that the Germans wanted to kidnap a young girl," our mother said.

"She's not just any girl. Kidnapping a member of the British royal family would have had enormous consequences. It would have been demoralizing to the entire country."

"I'm just so glad she's safe," Jack said. "Could you tell her how much I miss her?"

"You'll have a chance to tell her yourself," Little Bill said.

"She's coming back to Bermuda?" Jack asked excitedly.

Little Bill shook his head. "I'm afraid not." He paused. "But all of you will be seeing her, and her family. There has been a request made that your family travel to England to have an audience."

"An audience?" I questioned.

"Yes, that's what they call it when you meet with royalty," Little Bill said. "You will all be meeting with her parents, and another of her relatives has requested that you find time in your schedule to meet with her, perhaps for tea."

"A relative ... you don't mean the queen, do you?"

Little Bill smiled and nodded his head.

"The queen!" my mother exclaimed. "But I have nothing to wear!"

"I think a gown can be arranged," Little Bill said. "But first things first. George, how are you feeling?"

"I feel okay," I said. "Matter of fact, I almost feel ready for our next mission!"

Little Bill smiled. "The very answer I expected."